ICE & CROW

Scott R.S. Raphael

ISBN-13: 978-1-7381762-1-2

Cover design by: Scott R.S. Raphael

Dedicated to:

Chad

Table of Contents

Author's Note

SIX STORIES, ALL connected in some manner or another.

A bird.

A vision.

A race.

A child.

All touched by something supernatural. There is evil in the town of Reamish. No one knows that it's there until they're consumed by it. Then, there's no escape.

Ice and Crow is a short collection of stories written in early-2024. I'd like to give you a brief overview of each, hopefully to provide you with some insight into my mindset...or perhaps just to hear myself speak. It's funny. I rarely read "Author's Notes" or "Forewords," but I insist on writing them. If you've made it this far, congratulations! You're better than I am. Now, I'm going to inflict information upon you, whether you like it or not. I'll do my best not to spoil anything important.

"A Feast for the Murder" was one of the later stories written, and it was specifically designed for this collection, rather than operating as an independent tale. In many ways, it serves as a pseudo-prologue for what's to come and, particularly, for the final story, "The Hampburg Crow." Brief and brutal, its purpose is to give you a taste of what you're in for before you've gone too far. Hopefully, it will have you hooked!

"Lost in the Squall" is the oldest story in this book (by a few days). It was meant to be a haunting tale of a man guided by a ghost in a winter storm. As I was writing, it developed into a complex character study. I believe it is some of my finest work, but I'll let you be the final judge.

"Soul Race" is loosely based on a true story, with emphasis on the word "loosely." Inspired by a family member's accidental Christmas-season drive on a closed road, "Soul Race" grew out of the questions, "Why was the road *really* closed?" and "What if he hadn't been alone out there?"

I don't usually like writing from the perspective of children, because I don't feel that I understand them particularly well. But there was no other way to tell "A Fortress of Cotton." The "dark wind" is a concept that has batted around in my brain for years. I'm sure this is not the last we'll see of it.

I was reading a lot of Poe when I wrote "The Snow-Friend," and I was intrigued by his frame narratives as well as stories told by one character to another. And who can read Poe without wondering about one of his most common terror themes: being buried alive?

Finally, we come to "The Hampburg Crow," which is closer to a novella than a short story and takes up about half the collection. It would be easy to assume that the stories were always building toward this mysterious conclusion, but that is far from the case. In fact, the concept of the Hampburg Crow only came to me while I was writing "A Fortress of Cotton." Its mention in that story was a matter of a passing thought that I wrote in the moment. It was only after

I'd put those words to paper that I knew the underlying current that would tie all these stories together.

In the end, I've given you some answers openly. I've left others hidden throughout the text. And, of course, I've left some openings, in case we should ever like to revisit Reamish, perhaps thirty-two years from now…

A final note for my beloved beta readers. Yes, I followed through on my threat. But fear not: my perverse romance "Longer Than January" will find its way into a collection one day. It simply didn't fit here, as I'd always known but wished to deny.

I hope you enjoy *Ice and Crow.* From here out, you're on your own with the bird.

~ Scott R.S. Raphael
October 18, 2024, 4:20pm

ICE & CROW

"Go out alone and the crow will get you / Better stay home, or the crow will get you / He'll feed off your groans, and he'll tear you apart / If the Hamp-burg crow gets you, he'll eat out your heart."
~ anonymous, children's rhyme

A Feast for the Murder

HE SCREECHED FROM up on high, glaring down at a world that paled by comparison to the Hells he knew. One screech for the agony and another for luck.

He was a black mark against the sky, streaking across a haze of ugly, grey clouds that portended frostbite and car crashes on black ice. Those were souls for someone else to deal with. The bird had other intentions.

He soared above a man racing down the freeway; a stranger knocking on the door of a bereaved son; a decrepit and limping figure making his way home after a night in the forest.

They didn't appeal to him—not today.

The bird didn't think so much as he knew. His brain didn't speak; the future was something of a concept he was conscious of rather than one he planned for. The past only mattered for the lessons it had taught.

Don't fly too close to the sun: they'll see you in the light.

The bird plunged without warning, headed straight for the tunnels at the edge of town. He had never been there before but he could sense them, just as he knew the layout of this entire place. Past the university campus, over the Oublier Pub, and across the rows of crumbling pseudo-mansions that overlooked the lake.

The tunnels connected with the sewer system but had fallen into disuse some time ago. No one would see him and no one would suspect him.

He didn't notice the feather that was ripped from his tail during his descent. It fluttered behind him, caught in a gust of wind, and spun slowly to the earth. A scorched scar against the pale white snow.

He curled up just in time to avoid the ground and sailed into the tunnels. It was nearly pitch black in here, but he could see. He could always see.

The child couldn't see.

Sitting in a crook where the tunnel bent toward the water, head nestled deep into his snowpants. The child made the most awful wailing sound, deep from inside his tiny chest. He couldn't have been more than ten. All alone. Pranked by his friends and left in the dark. He didn't realize that if he turned the corner, he would find light and be able to race to safety.

It was too late now.

He had the aura. The bird could taste his soul.

Another screech. The caw echoed all around the tunnels over and over and over. The boy looked up in fright, his chest tightening, his entire body strained. He peered through the dark, squinting pointlessly. He couldn't see.

He would never see again.

The bird wasted no time tearing a hole in the boy's chest. The boy screamed out. Then his lungs were gone.

The tunnel echoed his cries, the last thing the boy would hear—the music to which the bird consumed his heart.

The heart let out one final beat in the bird's stomach. He felt overwhelmed by the aura of strength racing through him. Racing through him a little too quickly. Power wavered into fatigue. This was the worst part. The contrast.

Just a few more and he would be free.

But the winter was nearly done, and time fought to trap him for yet another year.

There was a girl in a cotton fortress, somewhere nearby. If only he could…

…but no. He needed time to regenerate, to recover himself.

It took a toll, to take a life. He had to allow the digestion to complete its cycle.

He soared from the tunnel without a look back or a glance at the feather in the snow. Home to give thanks. Home to sleep.

A few people saw him. A bus driver pointed. A detective dropped his notepad.

A moment later, the clouds turned dark, and the crow was lost amongst the black.

Lost in the Squall

"…TEMPERATURES OF MINUS…mi-nus…se…se…se…minus…"

The radio sputtered something incoherent that jud-dered around in Mason Wickwood's brain. He smacked the bloody old box once, twice, twenty-seven times, until his hand was redder than his son's ass had been that night he'd gone out joyriding with Tay and Rocky.

Tay and Rocky were dead now. Gone out in a nightstorm and ain't never come back.

His son—Jacko. Mason hated to remember his name.

Twenty-eight years in prison on an armed robbery charge. Two on the streets with a stick in his arm. Six years decaying in the dirt. He'd've been fifty-one if he'd had the sense to stay alive.

Mason had had the sense to keep alive. Seventy-two and kickin' like he was fightin' his way outta a box. And some days, he felt like he was. The eternal box.

Mason Wickwood kicked a shoe out of his way and realized he was wearing his slippers. Now, when had he put those on? He never put his slippers on un-til after seven o'clock at the dawdgam earliest and it wasn't near on…

…but hell, it was pitch black out. Pitch black but for the beads of crystal white cycling down from up on high. God's little missiles of spite. The frozen ashes of Hell.

The digital clock over the stove flashed a blue-green 00:00. Same in red from the microwave.

00:00 o'clock on the 0th day of the 0th month of the 0th year.

"Aw, you metherfreckin'..." Mason Wickwood kicked at the baseboard, forgetting he was in his slippers, forgetting that it was after dawdgam seven o'clock. He let out a howl and reached for the slipper. The slipper was to blame. He wanted to throw the slipper.

Couldn't bend down that far. Couldn't get his back to do what he freckin' told it to do.

Freckin' back.

Freckin' slipper.

Freckin' dawdgam seven o'clock.

Now Mason Wickwood was hunched over, half his usual height. Back didn't hurt—never hurt when he got all twisted and pretzeled up like this. Just wouldn't go back. Like a screw tightened a bit too tight. Didn't hurt nothin' for it to stay like that. Just wouldn't turn back no matter how you pulled or squeezed.

"Arlene!" Mason called at the stairs. He waited to hear footsteps padding along the hardwood upstairs. Waited. Nothing.

"ARLENE!"

Waited.

Nothing.

"AR..." Mason Wickwood grumbled to himself. No point in calling a woman who couldn't hear worth half a damn, couldn't walk worth another half, and didn't seem to care worth a third half. "Do a damn thing, do it yerself," he muttered, turning his back to

11

the wall and smacking into it once, twice, three times until, with a holler of—not pain, not release, just something that didn't feel quite right—his spinal column realigned and he was upright again. Upright as a seventy-two-year-old scoliotic could be after a stint in the navy, a stint in the mines, and a stint in the ER after he'd conked his neck, back, and head doing ninety-five in a sixty.

Knew he shouldn't'a been doin' it, too, but Mason Wickwood didn't much care after they found Jacko in the bush, naked, bruises up and down his arms, two frozen holes in his chest where they got him when he cheapo-ed out on the deal.

Arlene hadn't been in the car with him and she'd only come to visit him once. Just to cross her arms and say, "You're nothin' but a fool, Mason Wickwood. And if you weren't the fool I was stuck with, I'd've been on a plane to Buenos Aires in '93."

"Bitch," he muttered to himself now. Always on and on about Buenos Aires. Arlene had never been out of the U.S.A. in her life but she'd never shut her hatch about Buenos Aires. Said it was on account of the weather. Said it was on account of the people. Said it was on account of it being on a different continent from Mason Wickwood and his obsession over a nogoodnik she'd disowned the day he went away for pistol-whipping Fitzgerald down at the corner store over a few dimes and a packet of cigs. *Don't you remember Fitz, Mason? Fitz, who gave you a break when you were down on your luck? Fitz, who fixed the bills to let you make those tax claims all those years ago—at his loss? Fitz, who slipped an extra beer in your pouch every time you struggled to*

12

scrounge together enough pennies to afford a six-pack of Bud? You'd side with a nogoodnik like Jacko Wickwood, just because he shares your name, over Fitzgerald Duncan?

Didn't blood mean a dawdgam thing to that woman?

Freckin' Buenos Aires.

Only reason the old bitch wanted to go to Buenos Aires was on account of Javier Verga, half-man, half-horse, or so said the ladies down at the salon. Two years on a work program, and he didn't need but two weeks to win over every pair of tits in town.

Well, too late, Arlene Elisha Jackson-Wickwood. You locked in at nineteen and, unless you plan on makin' yer own way at seventy, yer in it for life 'round here.

Sometimes, though, it felt like she'd gone a long time ago.

It was cold in the house. Mason Wickwood didn't like the cold. Made all those little itty-bitty cells of skin stand up and prickle. He hated that prickle. He kept the house at eighty-three degrees all winter long just to avoid that ugly little prickle.

Mason Wickwood knew pain. He could take pain. He'd been stabbed by a bayonet for cripes' sake. Right on through his gut like he was made of paper. Hadn't cried, hadn't screamed. Took it like a man and would've stitched it up himself if his CO hadn't called him a freckin' fool and told him to sit the freck down and let the doctors do their freckin' job. He'd been trapped in a mine collapse for three days and had been the only one of the men who hadn't

13

whimpered in the night, sleeping amongst the rubble. And then there was the accident, of course.

But those little prickles on his skin—that wasn't pain. Those were little pinpricks from the Devil.

Mason Wickwood rubbed his arms. Scaly, dying flesh against scaly, dying flesh. Rubbed his hands across the tattoo of a pendulum that took up his entire left forearm. The one of the bird, finally set free, on his right biceps. More pain that hadn't bothered Mason Wickwood one iota.

The pendulum was for death. The bird was for life. The pendulum covered up the JW he'd once put there proudly.

And Arlene accused him of not taking Fitz's side.

He didn't take sides, Mason Wickwood.

Not since the navy.

Not since he'd tried to drown himself out because none of it mattered anymore.

Why was it so damn cold in here?

"ARLENE?" Nothing. "ARLENE? You open the door?"

Nothing.

He felt like he hadn't spoken to his wife in…he couldn't remember how long.

Hadn't cared for most of that time.

Now, he did.

He was cold.

He didn't need anyone to kiss it better when he tore his flesh and broke his bones.

But right now, seventy-two-year-old Mason Wickwood, clad in his slippers, not knowing what time it was—only that it was after dawdgam seven o'clock—back bent out of shape, father to a murdered convict, husband without a wife, just wanted someone to warm him up, make the prickling skin go away.

"Arlene?"

Mason ignored the pain in his foot, the tightness in his back. He pushed his way around the main level of the house.

The TV blared static. Just like the radio. Everything thrown off in the storm. Everything only half-alive. The blue and grey flickered the room into shadows and darkness and unnatural light. Buzzing, scratching at the air. For a minute, Mason Wickwood stared at the TV snow, lost in the squall. There was a remote around here somewhere, but he didn't know where it was. Hadn't seen it since—Arlene always turned off the TV after he went to bed, after she'd stayed up watching her infomercials.

Mason had called her a fool for watching those damned infomercials. "Only a fool would buy any of those nutjob products."

She never bought any of those nutjob products. Just liked the infomercials.

Even that was nutty.

Mason scratched at the prickly skin. It grooved under his paper-thin fingernails. Didn't like that. Felt like the little bumps were going to scratch right through the enamel.

Next room was the dining room. The table was scratched and small. They used to have a big table, one meant for parties and games and all the cousins who wanted to sit around, drinking a beer or a wine while talking about new jobs and old flames.

Mason couldn't remember the last time he'd had a visitor.

Most of the cousins were dead. Parents were long gone. Jacko never had a family. Not one they acknowledged anyhow. Used to be they'd have dozens over every Christmas. Then twenty, fifteen, ten, five.

Then just Arlene, sitting across the table, slowly sawing away at a piece of ham anyone with teeth worth a damn coulda bitten to shreds faster than she was cutting.

Mason'd come home one day and the table was gone. Replaced by some old ratty thing Arlene had traded for at a county show.

"Where's the dawdgam table?"

"I threw it away."

"Weren't nothin' wrong with that table!"

"It was too big. Look at the space we've got now. We can put a cabinet over there for all the plates. We can put a mirror over the figurines—mirrors are supposed to make a room feel bigger."

"The hell we gonna be spendin' that much time in the dining room for anyhow? We eat in front of the tube, piss in the can, and sleep in the bedroom. The hell we need more space in here for when ain't nobody's come in ten years."

Arlene had looked at him for a long time then. Not mad, just looking. Just thinking. Then she'd said, "Sometimes, you don't know what you need until you don't have it."

"ARLENE!" HE CALLED out again, quieter this time. He started up the stairs but it was no good. His knees didn't bend like they used to. He could take the pain. He knew he could take the pain. Didn't want to.

16

Hadn't wanted to for some time. They said he needed new knees after the accident. He remembered that but didn't remember why. Tried not to remember much.

He'd be fine, he said. He'd be fine. Had been until now, hadn't he?

Besides, Arlene wasn't upstairs. He'd've heard her walking around by now. She might've been old and light and dainty, but one thing Arlene Elisha Jackson-Wickwood had never been was a gentle walker. That woman would've left footprints in stone.

Only other place she could've been was the garage. No reason for her to be in the garage. She didn't do much in the way of handiwork. Didn't like spending time where it smelled like gas and sweat.

She'd tried to cleanse the garage with one of those fruity-flowery scent sprays a dozen or two years ago. Kept at it for days. Determined was that woman. Didn't do a thing. Open the garage door once and it all flooded away, but nothing could kill the pungent aroma of burning fuel. "That stuff's gonna kill us one day," she'd warned when Mason had left the door to the garage open one too many times.

He'd laughed at that. "If fumes was gonna kill me, they'd've taken me out in the mines."

Mason didn't remember much of the mines, aside from the cave-in. He remembered those three days well. Waiting in the rubble. Couldn't move much more than a few fingers on his right hand. His chest a few inches, just to breathe. The kids in the back—they cried out that they couldn't breathe, but they wouldn't've been able to cry if they couldn't breathe.

Turned out one of them actually couldn't. Dead on impact, they'd said. Rock to the skull, broke right through his helmet and pierced his brain.

Funny thing is, Mason Wickwood coulda sworn he'd heard that kid calling out at odd hours the whole time they were trapped down there. Like he'd screamed once and it'd echoed around for days.

MASON DIDN'T MAKE it to the garage door.

The moment he stepped into the front room, he heard a crash and a bang. He turned away from the flickering, snowy TV, from the renewed sputtering of a radio he'd've sworn he'd turned off. "…temperatures of minus…minus…se…se…se…minus…"

Another crash.

He saw the flicker of movement from the corner of his eye. His back seized up. His skin prickled even more.

Cr-crash. Cr-crash. Cr-crash.

The side-door of the house fluttered forward and back into the wall with each gust of frigid night wind.

Snow wafted and curled and sputtered to a halt in the doorframe.

There was a buildup of white on the linoleum. The door had been open a while.

Mason Wickwood never considered a burglar, a murderer. He'd've heard 'em. He'd've seen 'em. He'd've felt 'em.

Most of all, though, there couldn't've been an intruder. Not out here. There were no houses for miles. No major roads.

And most of all, there was nothing to steal. Not even his life.

18

Even Jacko's killers were long since dead, and his son's debts had long ago been paid with his life.

The only reason that door would be open was that someone had gone out.

"I went out," he mumbled to himself, unconvinced. "Took out the bins. Took out the bins…" Tuesday. Took out the bins Tuesday. It wasn't Tuesday, hadn't been Tuesday for a day, two—three?

Brought back the bins. He remembered bringing back the bins. Smacked him in the back of the calf, and he'd given them a good hard kick. Come back inside cursing and grumbling and looking for the alcohol for the flapping cut that had formed across the papery wrinkles of his skin. Used to be muscle there, used to be a man. Now they could feed him through a shredder and the blades might not even reach.

"Arlene!" he'd called up the stairs. "ARLENE!" Nothing. Like he hadn't heard from her in ages. Like she didn't care he was bleeding out all over the rug— the rug she'd got when she'd brought in that metherfreckin' table.

MASON WICKWOOD DIDN'T remember pacing over to the open doorframe, didn't notice he was there until it bounced off his back a few times in the gust. Cr-slap. Cr-slap. Cr-slap.

He smacked it back into the wall, then smacked it again for good measure.

Freckin' door.

In the freckin' way.

Makin' so much noise I can't dawdgam think.

"Arlene?"

The moment his slippered toe crept over the threshold, the wind sliced into his face. Instantaneous frostbite. A frozen relief of Mason Wickwood's face against the night.

Temperatures of minus…minus…se…se…se…minus…

It was wet, through the slipper, but not as wet as it should have been. The snow wasn't melting against his skin. He wasn't warm enough. He was cold all the way through.

One step, two.

Mason Wickwood cinched his bathrobe tighter around his waist. He didn't remember wearing a bathrobe, thought he'd been dressed. Never remembered owning a bathrobe. For pansies and rich prigs, bathrobes. Musta been Arlene bought him that bathrobe. But why in Hell had he put it on?

The snow gusted around his face, sharp little diamonds scritch-scratching at his cheeks and eyes. Little cuts, frozen shut. Slipping under his robe, nipping away at his nether regions. Didn't need that anymore anyhow, he spat in the snow.

"Arlene?"

No point in yelling; no point in crying. The night was too loud. Whistling shrieks of wind. The deep, screaming warble of the flecks of snow, bulleting by his ears. "Arlene?" He couldn't hear himself.

"Get back here now, Arlene. Yer too old for this. Yer not gonna make it home. You could slip or fall or…"

Aw, what good was it?

Even if she could hear, she wouldn't care.

She hadn't heard in so long. Hadn't listened in longer.

Mason Wickwood couldn't see a thing.

The snow was melting into his slippers now, like he was swimming.

How could the night be so bright and white and so dark at the same time? The little blades kept slicing against his eyes. The world was flickering lights. He was living in the infinite static of his TV.

Mason Wickwood stopped walking. He didn't know how far he'd gone. Couldn't see the house behind him. Probably couldn'ta seen it from five feet away.

Arlene couldn'ta gotten far. Couldn'ta gotten anywhere in this squall. Surprised he hadn't stepped on her, fallen flat on her ass, two feet outside the door. Surprised he hadn't done the same. Wasn't slippery, this snow. Stuck around, high and thick. Couldn't trudge through. Up and over, up and over.

White-speckled blackness to the left, to the right, to the back, and to the front.

Mason Wickwood didn't even know which way was home anymore. Shouldn'ta turned around. Shouldn'ta turned three, four times. The more he turned, the less he remembered. Was his head spinning or the world? Or was it just the storm, a tornado of icy dust?

He saw movement when he stopped moving. It was in front of him, wherever in front was.

A flicker on the horizon.

Clad entirely in white. There and then gone.

Much too large to be another snowflake.

An avalanche?

21

On the plains?

There it was again, in the corner of his eye. He turned. Nothing.

The back of Mason Wickwood's neck tightened, threatened to freeze in place. There had once been muscle to cushion his veins. Now, his flesh was a window.

The wind was no longer whistling, but something was. A low, haunting hum, eerily familiar yet oddly tuneless.

"How Great Thou Art"

There had been a time when Mason and Arlene would go to church, if just for show. Mason Wickwood had been an atheist since he'd realized God didn't talk back.

Arlene had never said what she believed and he'd assumed she'd believed the same. Didn't want to believe anything else.

Was always her idea never to miss a Sunday.

"Appearances," she said, while doing up her own with frills and laces and the most reverent salmon colour.

She knew verses by heart. Liked to quote 2 Corinthians 6:14. He never understood what it meant; never tried.

"WHEN I DIE…" She started so many sentences with *"when I die,"* and Mason told her every time he stopped listening right then, had no interest in talking about death, had seen and heard enough in the navy, in the mines, on the streets he walked in the dead of night. Didn't stop her. And didn't stop him hearing even when he didn't care to. "When I die, I want them to play 'How Great Thou Art' at my funeral. I feel like I hear it at every funeral."

"What good is following like a sheep?"

"The Lord is our Shepherd." She hesitated. "I guess you *were* listening, then."

THE FLICKER OF white in the distance was no longer in the distance. Mason Wickwood could sense it on his neck. Not the cold this time—something strangely warm, warming. Warming yet still causing those awful little pinpricks all across his skin. Even the weather—*"...temperatures of minus...minus...se...se...se...minus..."*— even the weather hadn't raised such a cluster of bumps.

"*Mason.*"

The nightwind knew his name.

"*Mason.*"

The nightwind smelled like lavender perfume and unbrushed teeth.

"*Mason.*"

The nightwind wrapped about his right biceps and curled long nails beneath his skin.

When he turned, there was nothing, but the wind still whispered behind him.

He turned.

And again.

And turned until he fell.

One knee embedded in the deep pile of snow. One slipper stuck to the ice.

She glided across the frozen glass that capped the banks, blending in with the infinite white across the infinite black.

Arlene.

23

She stopped in front of him and lowered a hand.

She was younger now, younger than Mason Wickwood remembered. Though, he realized, he couldn't remember the last time he'd seen her. The last time she'd looked her age. In his mind, she was twenty-seven. Had always been twenty-seven.

The humming stopped.

ARLENE SAID NOTHING.

Mason Wickwood did not reach for her hand.

Rather, she took his arm and raised him above the banks, into the heart of a cycle of snow. The place she touched sparked another flurry of bumps.

He could bang his toes and freeze his skin and take a clattering door to the back of the head, but nothing made Mason Wickwood scream—relinquish his manhood and scream—so much as those deathly pinpricks on his arm.

Arlene drew a finger to his lips and, there, more bumps arose.

Her finger slowly drew into his mouth. He could feel the bumps growing, his breathing inhibited. He couldn't breathe. Only stare into her empty, unblinking eyes as her finger in his mouth closed his throat.

He was silent.

She was silent.

Even the wind had gone silent.

Arlene leaned in close, whispered something in his ear.

It had been so long since he had heard her speak. He still didn't. But he understood what she was saying.

This time, when she took his hand, there were no bumps. His body had become numb. From the cold. From the pain.

From her.

Mason Wickwood did not feel his slipper become unstuck from the ice, or his knee unbend itself. He was merely following.

He had no desire to ask where they were going.

He wished only to tell her that she did not know the way. She couldn't. Not lost as they were, in the heart of a raging squall.

"Yer freckin' mad, woman," he couldn't say.

"Yer gonna wind up dead."

But he didn't like to think about those kinds of things. Not after the navy. Not after the mines.

If his tongue had worked, he still would have said nothing.

He wouldn't have been heard.

The piercing whistle of the wind, the haunting whish of the snow, the absolute silence of the empty night. It was impossible to be heard in the squall.

When he walked with her, it was as though he walked atop the snow. He didn't feel his body anymore. Just her grip. More the suggestion of her grip. Everything numb.

Arlene—like she didn't touch the ground, no matter how heavily she walked, stomped across the snow. Carried away in the bluster of the air. Like she didn't notice the chill, the pain—like she was number than he was.

By the time they reached the cave, Mason Wickwood wasn't sure whether he was awake or dead or somewhere in between. All he knew was, for the first time in miles, he saw something that was neither blistering white nor cavernous black. A grey chasm carved out of the night, topped with teetering snow, opening onto a hole in space and time.

The closer they came, the more familiar it felt.

The emptiness sucked them in.

A vacuum that promised to numb them even from the numbness they already felt.

Mason Wickwood did not want to go into that cave. He didn't care that he was dying in the night—even if he could not feel himself dying, he had to be dying in this cold. He didn't care if he was already dead. Maybe he'd died years ago, in the navy, in the mine.

Whatever he was and wherever he was, he was repelled by that cave, even as it sucked him in. There was something dead in there. Something wrong.

Control was Arlene's. She had never been strong—Mason recalled the days she had handed him jars with half-screwed-on lids and told him to open them for her. There were times he'd suspected she did it to make him feel like a man. After his accidents. After the years of physiotherapy he'd refused because he wasn't no bitch and he'd figure it out on his own. After he'd broken his dawdgam toe and his dawdgam back and his dawdgam sternum, trying to prove that his bones weren't so brittle, or that "osteoporosis" was just some big word doctors made up to make you think you were sick. So you kept coming back and paying the dawdgam piper.

Well, suck on this pipe, Dr. Lies.

Mason Wickwood stayed his foot at the mouth of the cave. The same way he'd stopped on his threshold just a few minutes earlier. No, hours. No—millennia?

Then, he'd felt obligated to cross into the bleak, to search for Arlene, wherever she might be. His slippers had gotten wet, then. Now, they felt dry, dried right out. He didn't have a choice. He knew that she was too strong.

Mason Wickwood resisted with what little muscle he still had until she'd whisked him like a feather from a windowsill and blown him into the deathly black.

A FLICKERING LIGHT, like a fire, but without a source.

As though they'd entered the pit of Hell.

In the mine, all they'd had was the dying sputter of a headlamp. The rest had been hidden or blown away. He couldn't see the voices but he could hear.

He couldn't hear anything here. Not with his ears. But there were sounds echoing around in his brain. The crackle of the flame, the reverberation of every step. Becoming greater and greater.

He felt uncannily alive in the cave, more alive than he'd been in his house, in safety. He'd been lost there, not sure of a purpose. There was no purpose here, but there wasn't meant to be. Just a cave away from the rest. A sanctuary for Mason, Arlene, and the end of existence.

The translucent white cloth that wrapped about Arlene's shoulders was clearer here. The snow long gone. His eyes no longer cut and sliced and ripped apart. Just a woman he'd known a long time ago in her fading gown.

When she wrapped the gown around him, the spikes receded from his flesh, back inside. Everything went back inside. The pain, the doubt. Mason Wickwood felt unnaturally calm, then.

Slowly, she laid him down, wrapping her arms underneath his for the first time he could remember since they'd been young. They never slept so close together. Not since Jacko. Not since well before Jacko.

Her pregnancy belly had been an excuse for them both to turn their backs. One they'd been searching for for a while. The twin bed became a queen became a king. There was no way to breach the subject of separate beds without saying what they both refused to admit they were thinking.

Her fingers felt like nothing as they clawed into his flesh. She had no nails, just bony fingers that slid between his ribs and took hold of his heart. Mason Wickwood could hear his heart beating in irregular time. A mixture between peace and confusion.

In the distance, the wind whistled a final note and blew the flickering light away.

It was impossible to say whether he was awake in the complete darkness. He could feel Arlene. He could not see her.

She was there and she was not.

Then, he was not.

IN THE MORNING, there was light.

The night before, Mason Wickwood had felt as though he'd walked a mile before Arlene took him to sleep, but he could see, the moment he opened his eyes, that they had barely breached the lip of the cave.

It was hardly a cave at all. A small alcove of dirt and rock, carved a few feet into the ground. Enough to hold a body or two. Less a shelter than a respite.

There was no sign of where that light had flickered from.

There was pain in his right hip, the spot he'd crushed beneath his weight for the entire night. Pain. Pain was back, numbness was gone. The only tingle that remained was in the frozen emptiness of his fingers and toes. He tried to wriggle his toes. The slippers had frozen solid.

His fingers—met resistance.

They were wrapped tightly into a cloth, pressed hard into a body. Trying to reach through it, through her.

Mason Wickwood pressed his elbow hard into the frozen dirt and shuffled himself away from Arlene.

She lay as still as she had in the night. As still as she had for an age.

Her face had rotted away with time. The black-and-grey remains of hanging strands of flesh coated a gaunt skeleton. Her gown was ripped, taken by birds and rats. Their life preserved in her death.

Her clothing was not white, as it had been the night before. Pink. Hints of salmon.

Mason Wickwood could not remember the last time he'd seen Arlene, the last time he'd spoken to her. He could not remember when she had changed. He was not surprised.

Natural.

In this state, she was natural.

She was as she was meant to be.

With Jacko.

She had disowned him once. They were owned together, now.

It was with surprising ease that Mason Wickwood pushed himself back to his feet.

He lost balance as he kicked one slipper away. Caught himself. Kicked off the other.

Slippers or bare feet, it hardly mattered in the snow.

And he never wore his slippers before dawdgam seven o'clock.

Besides, it wasn't much of a trek, was it? Dozen feet or so, few steps through the snow. Shouldn'ta let his robe get uncinched in the night. Damn feminine robe. 'Course it came open at the worst of times and left his bits and pieces turned to icicles.

Mason Wickwood stretched as he stepped back into the light.

The squall was dead. The day was bright. The snow was solid and coated in ice.

A gentle breeze plucked at the hairs on his arms and brought a few evil bumps to the surface. Mason Wickwood grunted and rubbed them away.

Needed to get back into the house. Away from here. Wasn't meant to be here. This place was for the nights. Wasn't nobody supposed to be out here.

The door flapped open and shut.

Mason Wickwood closed it and locked it.

Arlene shoulda done that. Shouldn'ta let it go flappin' about in the wind.

Coulda drawn attention.

Where was Arlene, anyhow?

He felt like he hadn't heard from her in ages.

Soul Race

JEFF ALBURQUERQUE HONKED loudly at the 1950s-style Chevy that was taking up both westbound lanes on Cappal Road.

Sunday drivers, he thought. *And on a Wednesday, too!*

Not just any Wednesday, either. Christmas Eve morning!

When everyone was either supposed to be home with their families or wasting away in sorrowful loneliness.

That was what everyone had expected Jeff to do: waste away. After all, he'd chosen the solitary lifestyle, sworn off the city in favour of the "peace and quiet" of a small town where everyone knew everyone. He hadn't counted on "everyone knowing everyone" meaning that he couldn't take a walk with the type of anonymity that he'd enjoyed in the city. But hell, at least the people were better out in Pennston Town.

Easier.

It had taken him a while to pick out that word, but once it struck him, he knew it was just right. The people were *easier* around here.

The local coppers didn't care if you took your can of Busch Light out to Bakewood Park on a hot summer's day. The kids walked home alone from school from five years old. The bartender didn't take your keys if you had one too many. You were only going two streets over, anyhow.

No, there hadn't been a drunk driving incident in Pennston Town in three years.

Folks knew the tricks. The coppers never bothered with the backroads. If you didn't drive drunk down Main Street, had you even driven drunk at all?

One thing Jeff had never adjusted to out in Pennston Town, however, was that *easy* sometimes equated with *slow*.

When he'd lived in downtown Caprice, everyone had operated at top speed. Taxis sped through crosswalks. Businesspeople walked so fast the sweat stains in their armpits dried from the wind they made. Even the kids were rushed through school. Jeff's daughter Sandy had been failing math, just couldn't figure out slopes. Had they held her back, given her remedial assistance? No, they'd shuttled her off to tenth grade with a "good enough and good luck."

It was too fast.

There was only so much head spinning and fast walking Jeff could do before he gave himself a heart attack—and he still swore to this day that that was exactly what had happened. His ex-wife Pat and his kids, Sandy and Mike—they'd all had a laugh at him together. Heads leaned in for dramatic whispers about his "massive coronary."

Oh sure, laugh about the day he'd almost died.

He'd been shovelling snow when he'd felt a tightening around his chest. It'd only lasted a few moments, but that was long enough for all the muscles in the top half of his body to constrict and cry out for release. Mike was convinced Jeff was making excuses so he wouldn't have to finish the chore. Pretty rich coming from a boy who hadn't cleaned his room in six years.

Jeff wasn't one to take a challenge without response, though. Even when a day had passed without further incident—when the pain was only a memory he projected back onto his body because he felt like he *should* feel something—Jeff had insisted on a medical checkup.

The doctors had never found any evidence of a heart attack, of course. But how likely was it that they find anything when they were too busy glancing at their wristwatches to glance at his charts?

It was hard to tell whether the snow-covered line was dotted in this area, but there weren't any police cruisers around. Jeff's tires skidded on the ice and snow as he sped up and pulled into the eastbound lane.

He made sure to take a good glance at the Chevy driver on the way by. Some old woman who looked like she'd died a few years ago. Jeff could never understand why old people went that slowly. They didn't have long left—why waste it?

Jeff might have left the city to slow down, but he hadn't left it to come to a complete stop.

After Pat had rolled her eyes one too many times, he'd packed up and left. Let her have the house. Please, God, let her file for custody of the kids. It was only two more years of child support until they were adults.

Jeff could work remotely. Focus on his hobbies. Maybe retire a little early.

The hobbies and savings dwindled when he discovered the local watering hole, naturally. But was he really living if he couldn't enjoy a few bevvies at the end of a long workday?

His twenty-year-old sedan sputtered. Jeff stepped harder on the gas but to no avail. He jogged over black ice, just caught the road again before careening off it. That was one more thing about city life that he'd taken for granted until it was gone: the roads were always cleared before the snow had finished falling. Out here, if someone didn't get driving early enough to create a tire track, you were going to find yourself trying to plough through a snowbank.

His tires spun quickly, but the car moved at half the pace it was supposed to. *At least still faster than Sunday Mary, back there.*

What he would've given for a better car. A sportscar, maybe, to attract a woman. He hadn't had a woman in a few years. He'd gotten a little too used to his solitude at first and then—the law of inertia, he called it. Once he was at rest, so he would remain.

The same had held him back on getting his desired car. He wished he knew more about engines or models, had listened more to his friend Dave's ramblings about his days at the shop. Jeff had committed a few months back to studying automobile history, to get some idea of what he was looking for. But then the TV had magically turned itself on every moment of free time he'd had, and once you're halfway through a twelve-season series, how do you stop?

There was a show on cars. He'd tried to watch that. Got put off partway through episode two when the narrator called a carburetor "fascinating."

"I'll be the judge of that," Jeff had said to his echo. Then, he'd turned it off and flipped to some police procedural from the '90s.

Jeff peered at the odometer. 190,000 miles. And he was pretty sure he'd done half of them over the course of the last twelve feet, the way the wheels were spinning.

He was so focussed on revving up that he almost missed his turn onto the highway.

He probably crossed a few solid lines, and the front of his car nearly struck the traffic barrier on the way by. He glanced in the rear-view.

No flashing lights. No honking horns. No dead pedestrians.

The holy trifecta of good driving.

As Jeff pulled onto the empty highway, he closed his eyes for a moment—just for a moment—to savour the peace that was the open road. Even at the best of times, traffic was sparse out here. He had a half hour's drive until the outskirts of the city encroached upon his freedom.

When he opened his eyes, he found today especially empty. Perhaps because it was Christmas Eve. Perhaps because God was rewarding him for his patience with that old bat back on Cappal Road.

But God was not in Pennston Town that day.

Jeff sped up as he blew by one exit, then two. Still not a car in sight.

The highway was lightly dusted with snow.

He slipped and skidded here and there, but with no one around to honk or pressure, Jeff kept his calm behind the wheel, focussing on the horizon, the trees that bent under the weight of the snow. The medians

36

reached to the sky in the resplendent glow of white, not yet tarnished by the black of rubble and gasoline.

Jeff became so lost in the beauty of the empty highway that he nearly didn't notice the flickering road sign he approached at twenty miles an hour over the speed limit.

Only at the last moment did Jeff bother to look up and squint through the daunting combination of winter haze and his astigmatism. He wasn't sure he'd read it quite right, but he'd thought he'd seen:

"ROAD CLOSED"

emblazoned in burnt orange.

Of course, this was impossible.

He was on the road right now.

At the next sign, he felt his certainty wane.

"ROAD CLOSED"

No chance it could be a coincidence…? Jeff glanced around, suddenly hoping to find another car. Specifically, one without flashing lights and a bullhorn telling him to pull over. Someone else to confirm that he was, in fact, quite in the right.

A third road sign, this one newer and less dulled by the elements:

"ROAD CLOSED"

Jeff pulled into the right lane.

There had been no blockade at his entrance, no notice he'd seen on the news that morning. No—he must have misread or misunderstood. Perhaps they had closed the road *since* he'd gotten on.

There would have at least been a sign by the on-ramp.

He thought back and remembered: pulling around granny; crossing the white lines…and at the entrance itself…

Jeff couldn't remember.

He hadn't seen any warning signs.

He hadn't looked.

Only a moment ago, he'd passed another entrance. He adjusted his rear-view and squinted into the distant past, not a thought for the road ahead.

A set of silver bars crossed the on-ramp two-hundred yards behind.

"ROAD CLOSED"

Jeff checked the eastbound lanes. Not a car in sight. Not a tire track in the snow.

A few beads of sweat appeared on the back of Jeff's neck.

It was okay—it was going to be okay.

He would simply get off at the next exit and…and…

And go where, precisely?

It would take him hours to get to Pat's place on the side roads. Jeff might have moved from the city to slow down, but not by that much. He couldn't survive the unnecessarily slow, like granny in the Chevy.

Slow was a choice.

Slow was peace.

Slow was *not* something he could bear to have thrust upon him.

Without realizing what he was doing, Jeff pressed his foot down on the pedal. Just a little, at first. Then more, then more. Until he was travelling at speeds dozens, if not hundreds, of miles over the speed limit.

His elbows shook. The sweat on his neck screamed as it flew away.

The further he could go without being caught…

And even if he were, he'd tell the officer that there had been no sign at his entrance. There hadn't been. Yes, he was sure of it. There *couldn't* have been.

A few dozen more miles and the road would be open again. Once he was part of regular traffic, no one would be the wiser. If they hadn't caught him yet…

But he'd thought too soon.

The sound came first, rising over the cr-chunk of gravel against tires.

A low hum that became a buzz that became the screech of a chainsaw against pavement.

At first, Jeff thought it was a siren. His eyes flashed for the nearest exit. Another three miles. Too far. They had him.

It couldn't have been a siren, though. There was no rise and fall. Just a rise. Getting louder and louder as the sound approached.

A few moments later, something came into view in the mirror. It zigzagged back and forth, with apparently no notice of the icy conditions or the storm of rocks that spat up in its wake. Jeff was so fixated on the violent disregard of the motorcycle, he barely realized that it left no tracks in the snow behind it.

The closer it got, the larger it became. Not just in the way any approaching object grew. No, this motorcycle appeared larger than any Jeff had ever seen before—taller than his twenty-year-old sedan.

And its rider grew, as well.

"Objects in the mirror are larger than they appear," he muttered, although it didn't sound quite right. *Appear larger than they are?* That wasn't it, either.

Before Jeff realized that the motorcyclist had breached his back bumper, he was already at the driver's-side window.

Jeff didn't lift the pedal from the floor as he looked up at the monstrous rider beside him. He could barely see above the car's frame. To obscure matters even more, a thick puff of black smoke spouted from the motorcycle and engulfed them both in a cloud of fire and ash. Even with the windows up, Jeff began to cough.

The wheel slipped. The tires lost traction against the ice. He was headed for the divider but he couldn't see where he was going.

Instinct told him not to stop, that he would regret it somehow.

His foot, however, obeyed logic and reason.

Even as he fought himself, he stepped down hard on the brakes. That was when the car began to spiral.

Jeff gripped tightly to the wheel, as though holding it steady could stay the car's momentum. For a moment, he had the absurd thought that he was like a child, trying to hold an airplane aloft by pulling with all his strength on the armrests. In a strange way, Jeff felt that he had even less control than that.

He was no longer driving—he'd given up that right when he'd stomped on the brakes.

The motorcycle was lost somewhere in the black—everything was black and grey. Distance didn't mean anything. He couldn't focus on any point of reference. There weren't any.

He was spinning his way both off the road and into the middle of the smoke storm.

Too fast. Too fast. Just like everything he'd wanted to escape in life, he was going *too* fast.

Then, he stopped.

There was no gradual slowing as the tires found purchase on the pavement or as air resistance pummelled him into submission.

One moment, he was spinning wildly out of control, on the precipice of death and an inevitable plunge into the deep ditches at the side of the highway.

The next moment, he was entirely still.

Jeff gingerly removed his clenched fingers from the steering wheel, pain searing through the muscles of his hands as he tried to shake them out, recover their original shape.

As he did this, he looked around for signs of the monstrous motorcyclist.

In the same way that the car's momentum had stopped out of nowhere, so too had the billowing of hellish smoke. The street was as empty as it had been a few minutes earlier. White and abandoned.

His car was angled slightly in the wrong direction, but there were no skid marks behind him, no circles in the snow. No tracks at all. As though he'd been dropped from the sky and into that spot. Or, perhaps, thrust upward from the depths.

He must have fallen asleep at the wheel, hit some black ice, maybe even flown through the sky for a bit—that would explain the lack of tracks.

Not really. Not on a straightaway road without hills or ramps to fly off.

41

But Jeff had never been an expert in physics. Who knew what was possible when Mother Nature procreated with the cruel workman of poor infrastructure and a seventy-year-old highway?

He shook his head—time to stay awake and finish the ride. Off at the next exit. No more of this playing with fate.

Perhaps the roads had been closed for a reason.

Jeff turned the key in the ignition. His sedan sputtered, spat, and stopped.

The gas gauge read nearly full.

The blinking lights told him that the car was on.

He tried again.

Sputter. Stop.

There went his hopes of not getting caught.

He was going to have to call for help and hope they believed his story of the unmarked entrance.

"Why did you stay on the road once you realized it was closed, Mr. Alburquerque?"

He thought for a moment, phone idle in his hand. *"I lost control of the car, of course."*

"For forty-two miles?"

Hm…

The motorcyclist from his dream!

"I saw a motorcyclist in distress—his engine was fuming. I was chasing him down to help him but he just kept speeding up."

Well, it would have to do.

Jeff opened his phone to search for the nearest tow, only to find that he was without internet. Dead spots in the middle of a major highway—it was unacceptable, really. What good were these politicians who did nothing for the safety of their citizens?

42

He was unsurprised to discover that he was equally without phone service.

Jeff grumbled to himself about taxes and phone bills as he tried to get his bearings. Nothing behind, nothing in front—just white, barren land, shrouded in a haze of snow and clouds. There were no exits in sight, no landmarks. He could only have been in the Valley.

He wasn't sure why they called it the Valley. There were no changes in elevation, no mountains. A Valley carved away from humanity, he supposed. An empty stretch of road that thousands travelled through daily but no one had reason to stay in.

The Valley would have been forgotten even by those driving through it if not for the years of horror stories.

The Valley was by far the deadliest stretch of highway in the country.

It had long been believed that this was due to little more than negligence and overconfidence. An empty road, especially at night, invited speeding and recklessness. Most of the crashes came from trucks changing lanes without checking their mirrors.

The thin lanes didn't help, making it all too easy to bleed into your neighbours.

And then there was the upkeep. Situated between two minor towns, neither had particular interest in taking financial responsibility for the road. It had fallen into disrepair about twenty years earlier, with potholes so deep they'd had to shut down one of the nation's most travelled routes for months.

After that, there had been intense pressure on the local politicians to do something, anything, to prevent a repeat.

That didn't mean that the Valley had become pristine, by any means. But the state and the towns had come to some type of behind-closed-doors agreement to fix at least the worst of the damage without digging too deeply into anyone's coffers.

That must have been what had sent Jeff flying through the air while he slept. Some pothole or crack that hadn't been packed with snow and ice.

At least he knew where he was. That was something. Although, anywhere else would have been better.

At best, he was a two-hour walk from the nearest civilization, and if he picked the wrong direction…

Jeff had not dressed for winter walking. He hadn't even brought a coat. After all, he'd only planned to be outside long enough to walk to and from his car. And Pat always kept her house so warm—he almost hadn't bothered with the sweater.

With the car giving up on him, he was surprised that the cold hadn't crept into the vehicle yet. In fact, it felt oddly hot.

That would only make matters worse once he stepped into the contrast of the cold winter air. It might only have been a few degrees below freezing outside, but by comparison to the inferno of the car, he was liable to turn to ice on the spot.

Jeff never got that far.

He grabbed the doorhandle and rustled through the drawstring backpack on the passenger's seat, looking for his wallet.

The first time that the door refused to open, he didn't look back, still searching through the bag. He jiggled the handle, felt around futilely for the lock.

After a few moments of grumbling to himself, he gave up on the wallet, slapped the bag to the floor. He turned to take the door in both hands, convinced it must have somehow frozen shut during the drive.

The second he turned around, his grumbling stopped, along with the rest of him.

Jeff's hand slipped slowly from the handle, collapsing to his lap with a thud. His mouth hung just an inch open, then another. His eyes widened.

He didn't realize that he wasn't breathing.

Despite that, he could still smell the rancid stream of smoke clawing its way through his every pore.

On the other side of the driver's side window was the motorcyclist, now shrunk to regular human size.

But he was not human.

His face was a pink and red mess of fleshy folds that looked like they'd been mashed together. The spaces for his eyes were holes in the melting mass. His mouth was a deep scar. He had no nose. In place of hair, flames sprouted from the figure's head, encircling him like a devil's halo.

The rest of his body was hidden beneath more traditional motorcyclist garb. Leather jacket and gloves. Jeans adorned with low-hanging chains. Slick, black boots that glowed in the winter sun.

His motorcycle was of the purest red that Jeff had ever seen. A red so deep that it could have been painted in fresh blood.

The car became hotter.

"Who are you?" Jeff finally managed to say after infinite moments of fighting his shaking jaw.

The window was closed, but the figure heard him anyway.

He smiled.

No, that wasn't quite right. The slit across his so-called face curled upward. Something viscous and puslike oozed from the corners of the slit. He said nothing.

"Are you the devil?"

Jeff didn't know why he'd asked. He just…knew, somehow.

But the figure shook his head, very slowly. Once to the left. Once to the right.

No.

"But you're with him."

Finally, the figure spoke. Or, at least, its mouth opened and Jeff heard sound. But he wasn't convinced that those things came in time with each other.

"He is with all of us."

"Not with me."

"More than you know."

Jeff's throat was dry in the heat of the car. There was a water bottle in his drawstring bag. At least, there *had* been. He hadn't seen that, either, as he'd searched for his wallet.

He hadn't seen anything at all. Just pieces of unseeable objects. Things he'd pushed aside without processing. Things he now thought he might not have been able to process, at all.

His mouth and throat clicked as he tried to speak. "What do you want with me?"

"*He* wants your soul."

46

Jeff shook, but he held firm. He couldn't let this beast feed off his fear. He couldn't let himself fall victim to it. He sat up taller, dared to look the creature in the holes of its eyes.

"Well, tell *Him* that He can't have it."

The creature's slit oozed again.

"My master never takes. He only deals."

"I won't make a deal with the devil."

"Then, you will never leave this place. This land is His. You will be lost here eternally. Closed off from the rest of your world. Don't think about trying it," the creature added as Jeff looked into the distance, squinting, as though he might be able to see relief on the horizon. "You won't survive the cold. There are temperatures here you've never felt before."

The instinct to challenge the creature was consumed by a deep internal pang that told Jeff that every word was true.

The road had been closed.

This wasn't his road.

This wasn't even his world.

He licked his lips carefully but couldn't wet them. "What do I have to do?"

"You must win." The demon raised a gloved finger and pointed in the direction Jeff had previously been going. "Civilization returns ten miles to the west. If I arrive first, then He will take your soul."

"And if I arrive first?"

Was that a smirk? The thing's face didn't move or ooze, but something sinister cut a shadow across his fiery head.

"If you arrive first, you will never hear from me again."

47

"My car won't start."

"That won't be a problem once the race has begun."

"Just let me go."

"I'm afraid I can't do that. You see—as I've mentioned, my master operates in deals. And whether you meant to or not, you've fallen into the heart of one."

"What deal?"

"So many questions. Your focus is misguided."

"Just tell me what the hell is going on?"

"Hm…Hell, indeed." He revved his engine and looked to the road ahead.

"Who are you?" Jeff repeated his earlier question, although he wasn't sure he wanted to know. "At least tell me who you are. Tell me who I'm up against."

"You're up against the world. You're up against Hell. As for me? I am merely the Collector."

With that, he was off, a shot that tore through the ice and left a scar along the highway.

There was no time for Jeff to think. He fumbled for the key and turned it.

By miracle, the car sprang to life.

Jeff whipped the wheel to the right and slammed down on the gas pedal, pulling the car straight onto the road.

The Collector had cheated. He'd taken a head start.

Jeff shook as much from anger as he did from fear.

None of this made sense. What had he done to deserve this treatment, this condemnation?

But he would have to address that when the race was done.

And to do that, he would have to win.

The motorcycle was just a speck in the distance. His twenty-year-old sedan wasn't built for racing.

But Jeff had a secret, one he'd sworn never to reveal. One he'd hidden so long he'd nearly forgotten it, himself.

It had been a youthful decision, driven by speed. Driven by a need to keep up with the hellish pace of city life.

A middle finger to the city.

A backup plan in case he ever felt like going wild.

A concept he'd pushed to the side when he'd chosen to slow down, realized that life wasn't meant to be lived full throttle.

His friend Dave had been a mechanic, looking for a project to make his mark on the world.

Jeff had been a young father, looking to recover his independent masculinity.

They had both been crazy.

Maybe Jeff still *was* crazy.

He unleashed a vicious howl into the dead, empty air. Then, he slammed down on the radio so hard that it fell away and crashed to the floor below. Beneath was a button, hidden from Pat.

If not for that button, he might've trashed this car ages ago, traded in for any type of newer model, no matter how bland or used.

But that button…

He pressed it now.

The sides of the car heated. It was hotter than it had been when the Collector had taken full control.

Thank God his tank was almost full.

Flames sprouted from hidden spouts on each side of the sedan.

49

Jeff laughed as the car picked up pace, screamed forward in pursuit of the motorcycle.

Fire.

The only way to fight fire was with fire.

This time, he embraced the sight of the motorcycle growing.

He was gaining ground.

The Collector didn't turn around, but he leaned lower against his handles, tried to increase his speed.

He couldn't outmatch Jeff's jetpack propulsion.

In the rear-view, Jeff could see the ice melting away, leaving a streak of water and scorched asphalt behind him. The water swayed with the shaking of the road, circling in whirlpools until it eventually refroze in the frigid air.

As Jeff drew even with the Collector, he took a moment to glance out the window. The flames that stabbed and sliced around the beast's head had grown frantic, doubled in size, but could not be extinguished. His gloved fingers tightened; his shoulders arched.

Slowly, the Collector turned his empty-socketed head to face Jeff. It was only for a moment that they were precisely even with each other, but in that moment, Jeff was sure he'd seen the corners of the slit begin to ooze.

Then, Jeff was away and ahead. He didn't know where the finish line was, but he had to be getting close. Part of him expected raucous applause from the bleachers of Heaven as he defeated the messenger from Hell. Another part of him knew that Heaven had no part in this and no place in the Valley.

He pressed down harder on the pedal, knowing he could push it no farther, willing it through the floor.

The Collector was now a speck in the rear-view, lost in the white haze of the horizon. The gas gauge was still half full.

There was something in the distance—he could see it now, emerging out of the bleak. A bridge, a cathedral. He prayed God could hear him from there.

Let me win, oh Lord, let me win.

There was something else, too, poking up from the centre of the road. As he neared, it grew, expanded, covered the entire lane. A finish line, a string of flags and bunting.

But then, why was it so low? Touching the road…

…coming at him.

Jeff veered hard to the left, foot never leaving the pedal.

Before him, a troupe of the damned approached.

Heads ablaze, motorcycles engulfed in the same black smoke that had invited him into this race in the first place. They sped in a line, blocking the lane.

No, the devil wouldn't take a soul without first making a deal, but that didn't mean He wouldn't cheat.

The motorcyclist in the lead pulled up on his back wheel with a cry that cut through the empty air. The others veered out to surround him.

Jeff pulled the wheel back and forth. There was no way around, only through. Something told him that through wasn't an option, either.

He cried out, praying that the world would hear him: "FASTER!"

The leading demon stared back at him with empty sockets. They faced each other head on, both revving, braced for collision. The black smoke surrounded them. The other demons were gone. It was just Jeff and this creature, now. Everything slowed down.

Too slow.

If he had to die, Jeff would have preferred to die then, as quickly as possible.

But in the slow, creeping moments that preceded the collision, he was forced to watch as the figure before him opened its slit. A sluice of blood oozed from the opening as something forced its way out. A head.

His head.

He careened toward his own screaming head. He closed his eyes. Braced for impact.

SOMEWHERE, IN THE distance, the Collector crossed the finish line.

*

ON THE BRIDGE above, they watched the race end, a few feet from the doors of the condemned cathedral. It had once been a Catholic mainstay. Now, it was a safe meeting place, the only place the state and city could gather. A new governor had laughed once: "I thought we were supposed to be separating church and state." No one else had laughed.

"It's never been so close before," said the governor.

"Were those rockets?" asked one mayor.

"I thought he was going to win," said the other.

"And then, where would we be?" The governor turned away. It was over now.

The mayors said nothing.

They didn't know what would happen if the Collector lost. They knew better than to want to find out.

"We're safe for another year." The governor closed his eyes.

"Is it worth it? Every year?" The mayor was new. He understood the importance, but he still held out naïve hope that there might be any other way. "He didn't deserve it."

The governor sighed. "The road was closed."

A Fortress of Cotton

THE SNOW MADE a scrunching sound under Annamae's hood and she giggled. It was just like cotton. Annamae had always loved cotton, the way it got stuck to the dry skin on your fingers and squeaked when you rubbed it close to your ear. She wanted to sleep in a bed made entirely of cotton—it would be like sleeping on a cloud. "You'd sink right through to the floor," Mommy had said. And Annamae had thought, *That's probably more comfortable than my stinky, old, rock mattress, anyways*. But Mommy had that serious look on her face that she made when she didn't feel like "having a conversation about it." So, Annamae hadn't pressed the issue. She'd learned that early on: don't press the issue. Like when Daddy had "gotten tired" and "gone to live with Ms. Deeley," Annamae's second-grade music teacher. Annamae had had an overload of questions then. She'd been sent to her room after two, while Mommy stayed in the living room, making heavy breathing sounds, thinking Annamae couldn't hear over the TV.

Mommy was happy today. It had been three months since Daddy had "taken a vacation." Four since Grampa had "gone a little questionable" and been put in that place with the thick, dusty smell and women in pink-and-teal uniforms who called Annamae "Sweetums." Six since Gramma had "gone to Hell. Probably in one of those very handbaskets she made for kids in Africa while her own had to…" Mommy had noticed Annamae listening in on her phone call then.

Today was the first time Mommy had seemed happy in a long time. It had been so long, Annamae had almost forgotten that Mommy could smile in a way that wasn't tired.

There had been no warning.

Yesterday had been a normal day. The last day of school before the holidays—now at Annamae's new school, the one she'd fought against but had been told she had to go to, because Ms. Deeley was a "c-word" who didn't want to see Annamae anymore. Mommy hadn't told Annamae what the "c-word" was, but she was pretty sure it was the thing Mommy had yelled at God from behind closed doors, the last time she'd prayed, three months earlier.

When Mommy woke Annamae up at seven a.m., she thought she was in trouble. Mommy liked to let Annamae sleep in these days. She told her daughter that it was because she was a "growing girl" who "needs to sleep to get big and strong." Mommy must have also wanted to get bigger and stronger.

Not today. She'd rushed into Annamae's room, singing their favourite Taylor Swift song, with two bowls of super-sweet, sugary cereal. The type she'd told Annamae she was only allowed to have on special occasions. The type she always refused to buy at the store.

The first day of winter break was a special occasion, then. It hadn't been before. It had just been another Saturday, where Mommy and Daddy would "talk" in the bedroom while Annamae watched reruns of cartoons and ate Doritos straight from the bag.

Today, it was, "What are we going to do first? Christmas shopping? Or we could go to the movies? Or have lunch at McDonald's?"

It all sounded enticing. Annamae loved the mall at Christmastime, watching people rush around and look stressed for no reason while "Jingle Bell Rock" played out of time with their frantic running. There was a new Christmas movie out about a reindeer who couldn't fly. And McDonald's was her favourite— she'd received many a confused look for her love of ordering a McFlurry in the winter. But what could be better than more ice and snow during the best season of the year?

Which is why she didn't think twice before answering: "I want to play outside! We can build a snowman and make snow angels and play hide-and-seek and build a fort and—oh! Oh! We can play I'm the King of the Castle!" That had always been her favourite game with Daddy, where they would find a snowbank and race to the top. And whoever won got to be "king of the castle." Annamae used to say she wanted to be *Queen* of the castle, but that was before Daddy had taught her that king was *better* than queen.

Mommy had been smiling and nodding until the mention of that game. She tried to keep the smile but flinched when Annamae mentioned it. "Why don't we start with snowmen and snow angels and see what time it is?"

Annamae wanted to start with I'm the King of the Castle, but Mommy had always told her that it was better to "save the best for last." Yes—she would have all day to look forward to building a fort and playing I'm the King of the Castle.

The snowman watched them now, as they made snow angels in an otherwise pristine patch of snow. Mommy had driven to a field that gave them plenty of space to move around. It was a little outside the town centre, nowhere near houses and buildings. In fact, outside the occasional passing car, they were the only ones around.

The snowman's hat had blown away in a gust of wind and been lost to the streets, but his carrot nose was lodged firmly in place. The sun now cast a shadow of the nose right across their necks as they lay in the snow.

Annamae swam through the cotton around her ears, fast then slow, making sure to make the best impression ever. She pictured herself sleeping there forever, her bed of cotton. Another frigid gust cut across her cheeks. She'd started to lose feeling in her face a while ago, but she'd told Mommy that she felt fine. She didn't want to have to go inside—not for one second.

"We have to be careful, now," Mommy said, pushing up on her hands. She was careful not to smudge the outline of her snow angel. "You know how we get up so we don't ruin the angel, right?"

Annamae remembered this lesson from several winters ago. Mommy was an expert at snow angels. They were Mommy's favourite part of winter. "We always leave a part of ourselves behind, everywhere we've been," Mommy had once said. "Usually, you can't see it or feel it—you just have to know it's there. A snow angel—it's like that. You leave yourself behind and you just stay there."

"Until it melts away," Annamae had said.

Mommy had smiled a little at that—not a happy smile. Something with distant thought behind it. "We never really melt away."

"Okay, just like I taught you," Mommy said now.

Annamae shuffled up onto her hands and slid her bum a few inches up the angel. She was careful not to disturb the edges. The snow was nice and deep here. Their imprints would last a long time, if she did this right. The first few times, she'd ruined her angel, but she'd learned years ago that it wasn't "worth crying over" because she could "always make another one."

This one was perfect, though. She'd never made a snow angel this perfect. She wanted her perfect cotton bed to remember her forever, just like that.

Annamae was cautious, as she got to her feet, not to put too much pressure on the snow below. Avoiding boot prints altogether was almost impossible, but the lighter you stepped, the less noticeable they were. She bent her knees a few times to get momentum. Then, with a big leap, she and Mommy simultaneously broke from their snow angels and landed a few feet away.

"Perfect," Mommy said as she turned back to look at the angels.

"Take a picture of me with my angel!" Annamae rushed to the side of her creation, keeping enough of a distance so as not to disturb it.

But Mommy shook her head. "I left my phone in the car."

"Go get it!"

"Hush, Sweet." She used to say "Sweetums," like the ladies at Grampa's new home, but had stopped when she'd heard it out of someone else's mouth. "It wouldn't be right."

"Why not?"

There was that weird smile again, the thinking one. "Some things are only meant to be temporary."

Annamae was about to ask another question, but Mommy was already walking away. That was the other thing she'd learned long ago. Sometimes, instead of a serious face, Mommy would simply walk away when a conversation was over. Annamae jumped through snow that came up to her knees, struggling to catch up to even Mommy's slowest footsteps.

"Can we play a game now? Can we play…" She was going to say I'm the King of the Castle, but Mommy interrupted. Even though she always told Annamae never to interrupt, Mommy was the exception to the rule. She'd made that clear long ago.

"How about hide-and-seek?" She gestured vaguely to the trees and rocks that littered the field on the opposite side of the street. "I'll cover my eyes and you go hide."

Annamae wanted to protest, but Mommy had already started counting.

"But you haven't covered your eyes."

"I need to make sure you get to the other side of the street, Sweet. Then, I'll close my eyes."

Annamae made a face at that. She was big enough to cross the street without being watched. She did it every day on the way to school. It didn't matter that that was a side street with minimal traffic and a crossing guard. She was eight years old. She could cross any street she wanted, any time she wanted.

59

But if Mommy was going to treat her like a child…

Annamae paused at the edge of the road and looked both ways. Then, she leaned forward and looked each way again, as dramatically as she could. She glanced back at Mommy, still counting but too far away to hear. Annamae nodded: *You see? I know what I'm doing.*

She even jogged as she crossed, kicking up dirt and slush that seeped its way between her snowpants and the top of her boots. But she couldn't let Mommy know. Not when she was trying to prove that she was a big girl. On the other side of the street, she turned and opened her eyes wide: *See? Told you!* Mommy was much too far away to see her facial expression, but Annamae was sure she'd gotten her point across. Mommy even nodded once, and Annamae was pretty sure she saw a smile—a real one this time, not one of those ones that actually meant something else.

Finally, Mommy covered her eyes, and Annamae rushed away into the trees.

From the distance, the evergreens looked like a sparse collection of pipe-cleaners. They were thin and tall, straight up and down. They looked emaciated and weak. It was funny, Annamae thought, how fat trees looked healthier than thin ones, but fat people were "overindulgent pigs," according to Daddy. She'd had to ask for clarification, but "pigs" were bad in this case and "good when they're pork." In moderation, of course.

Once she was in the miniature forest, it didn't feel so sparse anymore. The trees might not have been thick, but they leaned together, swaying off-balance under the weight of the snow. Only pinpricks of sky peeked through, giving the impression of early evening, although it was only one in the afternoon.

After a few steps, Annamae heard a rustle, saw a flicker of black out the corner of her eye. By the time she'd turned, it had gone.

A cougar, she thought, not entirely sure why. She'd never seen a wild cougar. She'd been told once at the zoo that there were no large wildcats in all of Morosa County, and the only animals to fear at nights were the coyotes and the Hampburg Crow. But she'd seen a cougar in a textbook and now it was all she could see. Anger behind its glowing yellow eyes. A string of drool hanging from its lower lip. Superimposed sabretooth tiger teeth.

She would go no further into the forest—it had become a forest in her mind.

She would have to hide right here and wait for Mommy to find her. The trouble was, right here was in the large-mouthed opening to the forest, so visible that a blind man could spot her from a distance.

She could hide behind a tree…maybe Mommy would walk right past without turning around, and then she could slide to the opposite side of the tree and keep the game going all day! The moment she ducked behind the first tree—the closest to the open field behind her—she knew this simply wasn't going to work. Even though she was a small child—always stuck in the first row for class photos, never allowed to be the goalie for gym hockey because she couldn't cover "even a corner of the net"—she was still too large to hide behind these emaciated trees. Her snowpants stuck out one side, her boot the other. Her hood alone was so wide that it stuck out on both sides.

For a moment, she thought about burying herself in the snow. Then, Mommy would walk right over her and never notice. She dropped to her knees and dug away a few inches of snow, letting it pile up behind her.

But that pile gave her a different idea.

I'm the King of the Castle.

She'd often heard Mommy talking of "killing two birds with one stone," but she'd never understood. Why would she want to kill a bird—unless it was that evil Hampburg Crow? Suddenly, it made sense.

The birds were her games, and killing was fun, somehow.

If she built a fort, hundreds of feet higher than the little mound behind her, she could hide inside. And when Mommy found her—or when Mommy said "come out, I can't find you," because of course Annamae would never be found in such a brilliant hiding place!—she would already have a fort ready for her favourite game.

She worked quickly, packing snow down hard into a pile. She wouldn't have much longer before Mommy started looking. She jumped into the hole she'd created to continue padding the wall. Annamae was hidden from sight now, and she would use that bulwark to buy her time as she built the walls around her.

She started on the side walls, grabbing snow from all around, careful to keep her gloves from appearing around the edges of the wall.

She giggled at her brilliant plan and quickly covered her mouth.

Annamae was fortunate that a truck passed by and blared its horn at that very moment, or she might have been heard.

She was so engaged in her work that she didn't notice the time passing. Soon, the back wall was complete. Then, she realized her problem. She couldn't access more snow for the roof! There was no way out without blowing her cover. She was going to have to use the snow from inside.

Annamae had been so careful to build nice, thick walls, just like Daddy had taught her about from his construction job. Big walls hold up. Thin walls break down. But she could fix the fort after Mommy found her.

Carefully, she brushed as much snow as she could from each wall, packing it into place above her. Clumps of icy cotton kept falling away, barely missing her face. When the last snowball was finally in place, Annamae carefully lowered herself from the walls. *Don't touch anything*, she thought.

Despite all her effort to stay hidden, she hoped Mommy would find her soon. She was getting tired and didn't want it to get so late they couldn't play I'm the King of the Castle. She also had to pee, and *that* was "a whole process"—one of the few things Mommy and Daddy agreed on.

The world was a mystery to her now. Normally, she might have been scared in a closed, darkened space, but mostly, she was glad that she was safe from the cougar—it would never think to look here!

63

And there was still a little light. She'd left a tiny slit in the roof of her fort, a place to look out to see if someone were coming. She couldn't make out much more than white daylight and flashing blue-and-red, though.

She listened carefully for the sound of footsteps. The trees rustled. A bird cawed.

Annamae jumped at a loud THUMP that made the weak foundations of her fort vibrate and threaten to collapse.

After a few moments without another sound, she realized that it must have been a clump of snow, falling from up on high.

It was warm in the fort and now it was getting warmer. It took a moment for her to realize that she'd lost control of her bladder when the snow had fallen. She felt strangely good for a moment, comforted in the heat of her own urine. Then, the cold kicked in.

Annamae shivered. She considered giving up the game. But she'd done so much work, come so far.

Mommy would call out soon. She had to have been hidden here for a whole day now, almost! At least, it felt like it, even though she could still see the same old daylight poking through the hole in the roof.

Annamae sat back and tried to get comfortable. Her wet underpants didn't feel quite so cold when she was sitting in them, pressed down against the ground. She tested the wall behind her, if it would hold. She leaned back. A little rub of cotton behind her ears. No movement. It was secure. She put a little more pressure backward. She was safe to put her whole weight on the wall.

No collapse. Still a great view of the hole.

With the padding of her snowsuit and snowpants, it was like she was lying in bed. The cotton bed she'd always wanted. When Mommy found her, she could tell her, once and for all, that you wouldn't slip down and end up sleeping on the floor. It was the most comfortable she would ever be!

*

WHEN ANNAMAE AWOKE, it took a moment to realize where she was. It was nearly pitch black; there was something hard and sharp on her face. The cougar flashed through her mind and, for a moment, she thought that its tooth was lodged in her cheek as it played with its food, waiting to tear her apart. Wet drool dripped down her face. Her heartbeat raced.

On instinct, she reached up to swat the animal away, in some dazed sense that it might help. To her surprise, it did.

The hard, sharp, wet object flew away. She had won. Everything was still dark, but she was alive. And she needed to run. Annamae leapt up and immediately fell back down as she made contact with the wall of her fort.

The snow toppled down around her, burying her whole.

Snow.

It was just snow. Not a cougar's tooth and drool. Everything was just snow.

Annamae heaved a clump of ice off her chest and breathed deeply.

Relief. She was safe.

But why was it so dark?

Had she gone blind? No, she could see her red gloves waving in front of her face. Not that they looked very red. More of a bleak grey against a darker grey.

Annamae squinted around what remained of her fort until her eyes adjusted to the shades of darkness. Her fort was still more or less intact, with just a few new holes in the roof. From what she could make out of the world, it was nighttime.

In the winter, night lasted forever, but Annamae had never remembered it coming in the middle of the afternoon.

It had to be at least five o'clock, maybe later. Four hours—and her mother hadn't found her. Who knew how long she might have been looking, calling, walking overtop the mound in the middle of otherwise untouched snow.

Everything was silent now, except the cool rustle of wind over the hole in the roof.

"Mommy?"

She waited. No response.

"MOMMY?"

Something flickered on the other side of the hole. It was difficult to make out against the black.

The cougar?

No—it was too clear to be the cougar. It looked like…

There it was again.

Translucent, like it was barely there at all. Then, it was gone.

Like the wind had a body, a series of dark specks. It wasn't snow. Something was there, looking for her. Something incorporeal. Reaching.

66

"Mo…" She caught herself. Whatever that thing was, she wasn't sure she wanted it to find her.

A voice whispered in her ear, "It's okay."

Annamae screamed and jumped away. She struck the wall of the fort and brought the rest of the structure clattering down, an avalanche of ice and snow.

Annamae tried to stand but was struck on the head. Her leg was trapped in a mound. Her arm had caught a hidden tree root and her coat began to tear.

"Help!" she cried, searching wildly for the source of the voice. Not knowing if she wanted to find it.

The voice had been clear, echoing, sweet. It had sounded like it was trying to help. But there was no one around.

She couldn't get up. She was going to be crushed under the snow. This wasn't like cotton, at all. She wasn't falling through it. It was falling through her.

She felt a tight grip around her left wrist, but she couldn't see where it came from. She couldn't even see her wrist. The grip tightened. Annamae screamed.

There was a sharp tug. Her shoulder pulled in a direction it wasn't meant to go. The rest of her body resisted, feeling like a dead log being yanked by a fishing line.

Her glove scratched against the snow and pulled off as her hand broke free. Her head was next to breach the surface. Then, slowly, the rest of her followed.

Annamae's screams had turned to tears. She could barely see in the darkness and now everything was blurry. Her face was freezing from the night wind against the water tracks of her cheeks.

67

"Shh…" the voice whispered, not unkindly but urgently.

Annamae tried; she really tried. It wasn't so easy to stop crying on command. She swallowed back sobs, did everything she could to take a deep breath that just wouldn't come—breaths that sliced at her lungs like icepicks.

A gentle force pushed against her face, wiping at the tears but unable to push them away.

Annamae was scared to turn around. Whoever— whatever—had her was still gripping her arm, fingers digging tightly into her skin. It didn't feel entirely unfriendly. But it didn't feel right.

She pulled away, but the force didn't let go. She pulled again. "Let…me…go…" She managed to get the words out between heaving breaths.

"Annamae, Sweet."

She stopped. She stopped breathing altogether.

Mommy.

Annamae's shaking slowed to a stop. She turned to face the woman.

But it was not her mother.

In her mother's place was a figure that looked something like Mommy. But it wasn't.

Not entirely.

The same height. The same figure. The same posture.

But her chestnut-brown hair was missing. Her eyes neither sparkled nor suffered. Her clothes were gone.

Every colour and nuance was erased.

In their place was the mere outline of a woman. Everything else was coloured in sparkling silver. She was a shining light. A figure of fantasy. A gleaming, faceless glow against the night.

"M-mommy?"

"Shh," the figure repeated, drawing the outline of a finger to the outline of her face.

She bent down close. Annamae pulled back but the figure still had control over her arm.

"Annamae, you need to listen to me."

It was Mommy's voice, but it wasn't Mommy.

"Who are you?!" she screamed, now using her other hand to try to free her arm.

"Annamae, you need to be quiet. I'm here to help you. I'm not your mother, but I am, in a way. So, you need to listen to me."

"What are you? Who are you? LET ME GO!"

"Annamae!"

The little girl had never heard a word sound so much like a yell while barely rising over a whisper.

After a moment had passed, the figure went on, slower, quieter, softer: "I'm a snow angel, Annamae. I'm your mother's snow angel. The one she made earlier today. And I'm here to keep you safe. You're not safe out here in the night."

Annamae took a moment to process. It was fantastic. It was crazy. But hadn't her mother always said that you left a part of yourself behind everywhere you went?

A pristine outline of her mother.

A snow angel.

"Are there cougars out here?"

Annamae could not tell whether the snow angel was smiling or if she was making one of those thinking faces that Mommy sometimes made. "I wish there were only cougars to worry about out here."

"Am I going to die?"

"Not if we hurry."

"I saw something…when I was in the fort."

The snow angel took a deep breath. Wind fluttered around her face.

"Come on." She kept hold of Annamae but no longer needed to drag her. They started across the field, toward the road.

"What are we running from?"

"The thing you saw."

"What was it, Mommy…I mean, snow angel?"

The snow angel paused, looking away, thinking. They were getting close to the road now. "His name is Frost," she said finally.

"Like Jack Frost?"

"In a way. And just as cruel."

"What will he do if he catches me? Will he take me away? I don't want to be taken away."

"Sweet." The angel looked around. She had no eyes, but she could see. "What I'm about to tell you is something very adult, but I need you not to be scared, okay? Can you be a big girl for me?"

Annamae nodded. For a moment there was silence, and she thought the angel might not have seen her nod.

Then, the angel said, "Do you remember when Marty the Mouse had to go to the big block of cheese in the sky?"

"I know what death is, Mommy…I mean, angel."

"You understand that, when you die, you don't come back."

"But little pieces of you stay behind, everywhere you've been."

The angel went quiet a moment. There was a quiver in her voice, a weak breaking that painted her next words: "Trust me, Sweet, when I tell you that it's not the same."

"Is Frost going to kill me?"

The angel never had time to answer.

Across the darkness of the field, a cold wind blew, carrying with it a fleeting translucent vision. Specks of darkness across the night. An unseeable being in pursuit.

The angel let go of her arm. "Run!"

Annamae and the angel raced through the snow, the angel gliding along the top while Annamae trudged through knee-high mounds and tried to stay above the ice. Her pants weighed heavily from where her urine had frozen solid. Her thick, ripped coat fought against the wind.

"I can't run as fast as you!"

"You need to try! You need to go faster!"

They were nearly to the roadside now.

"You need to get somewhere safe," the angel called as the wind did its best to erase the sound of her words. "Find houses. Knock on doors. Get inside. Anywhere. Before…"

That was it.

The translucent figure attacked from the side. In a gust, he blew through the angel.

She exploded in a supernova of silver, sprinkling in all directions. Like a dirty boot clattering through the pristine outline of a perfect snow angel.

The snow angel became shards of the night, figments of dying snow cast in all directions.

Then, she was gone. Erased by the wind.

A truck horn blared. A police siren wailed. Her mother screamed, somewhere in the distant past.

"Mommy!" Annamae called out. But it was over, and her mother was long gone.

Annamae stopped. She hadn't meant to but she'd had to. She was alone, lost, unable to fend for herself.

In the distance, the figure called Frost pursued.

Annamae summoned whatever energy she had left to run, trying to force the involuntary tears back into her face. It was so cold.

When her boot caught on the lip of the snow's surface, she plummeted face-first to the ground.

She was stuck. Couldn't get up. She needed help, the way the angel had helped her up last time.

She needed an angel.

Without thinking, Annamae threw herself as hard as she could onto her back. She began swimming. Her arms and legs flailed rapidly. It couldn't be a perfect snow angel, but it would have to be enough.

Frost approached.

She closed her eyes.

Come on, come on.

The rubbing sound screeched against the back of her hood.

Come on, angel. Come to me. Save me from Frost.

She saw it coming above her, translucent specks spiralling around her eyes.

All she could think was, *I don't want a cotton bed anymore.*

"POOR KID, NEVER stood a chance out here."

Detective Craven Ackersley tapped his cigarette and let the wind take the ashes wherever it pleased.

"What's the story, Li?" Detective Anaïs Piers didn't want to look at the body until she had to, was turned to the road and watching the cars go by. Two deaths within twenty feet of each other, on the same day. Although, the kid's body hadn't been discovered until morning.

The coroner, Tina Li, didn't bother to look up. "Looks like it's what it looks like. Might need an autopsy to be sure, but I'm calling this one plain and simple hypothermia. The frost got to her."

"Not related to the Hampburg case. That's a relief, I guess."

"Looks like she relieved herself, too." Ackersley took another long drag on his cigarette. Li glared as speckles of ash threatened to shower over the body.

"Be respectful, Ack."

He shrugged. "Not like she can hear me."

ACROSS THE FIELD, Annamae watched on. She didn't understand.

They were talking about her like she was dead, but here she was.

Ackersley—he seemed rude, uncouth, but she liked something about him. Maybe it was that he didn't back down under pressure like Daddy used to. Maybe it was that his jawbone was hard and his cheekbones deep, like he'd sunken into himself a long time ago. He was funny-looking, but in a good way.

She liked that he was going to take care of her. More so than Piers. She reminded Annamae of Ms. Deeley, with her hair up tight and her blonde ombre.

They had come to help her. But she didn't need help. She was here, alive and well. It seemed a little funny that her arms were silver and glowing like the snow angel, but she figured that must have been the effects of a long night. She was tired. She'd been tired all day, like when she'd fallen asleep in her fortress of cotton.

She wasn't the one who needed help.

Deep inside, she knew there were others. Kids like her who got trapped in the frost. They were the ones who needed her.

She would find them and guide them, when the darkness fell. Just as her snow angel had for her. Like Mommy had tried to.

Annamae wondered where Mommy was.

Mommy was gone. But pieces of her would never die. That was how it worked. That was what Mommy had told her.

And in the same way, pieces of Annamae would never die.

Those detectives didn't understand that.

It wasn't the same, but in some way, she would always live on.

The Snow-Friend

For a moment, I think there's a twinkle in his eyes. Then I realize it's nothing more than the glimmer of a distant streetlight off a snowflake. There's a mechanical methodology to the way he packs snow. Years of factory work, I suppose, creating an ingrained routine. I've never before seen a man with the ability to focus on something so repetitive without losing interest or time. A woman, yes. But never a man.

But then, Livio Claudius Righetti is far from a usual man. For one thing, he speaks with a lilt of a Norwegian accent despite his Italian name and purely American upbringing. He also doesn't seem to recognize the cold. It has to be five, maybe ten, below zero and here he stands, in little more than a Rhapsody of Fire concert tee and worn-down sneakers. The only sign he shows of being aware of the mounds of snow around him is his rolled-up pant cuff. And even then, just one of them.

Livio has more important things to do than to pay attention to little matters of health and comfort. He's a man of action, certainty, force. I might have respected him, in some other life. Even some other day. Had I not met him this day, under the darkest of circumstances, then perhaps...

I don't care to think any further on that. It's not productive. What is simply is. It's too late for self-doubt.

How I wish, though, I had waited. There's no good in seeking answers on the day a man's father is laid to eternal rest. Raymond Righetti, an unassuming banker by trade. A man of the people, of the world. Known to most for his travel guides. Known to his family for the wealth he would not share. Raymond Righetti had left this world on Tuesday, December 17th, in the year 20—. On that day, he didn't have a penny to his name.

His wife was twelve years dead. His son, Livio, would inherit nothing.

In my years of investigative journalism, I've had only one goal: to find the man who upended my life. I shrouded that, of course, beneath a guise of professionalism. A woman must, to be taken seriously. I put in my time, wrote my tripe about abused animals, stolen government funds, the curious criminal allegations that surrounded that damn crow.

It was all an exercise in patience as I built my case, prepared to obliterate the man responsible for my father's disappearance. And then, that opportunity was gone.

I don't believe that Livio is unsympathetic. There's something in his face, as he packs a ball of snow together and glances at me. It resembles dismay. It isn't dismay. But it resembles it. He wishes things had turned out better for the both of us. But our fathers are gone and we are left to make our own decisions. We both made errors.

Livio sighs and begins to shovel jagged shards of ice from a mound beside the back gate. Once an impediment, now a tool. He uses the ice carefully to mould the snow. Forever an artist, even though his dreams long ago failed.

"I wanted to be a sculptor."

Yes. I know that. Finding the rejected applications to a variety of art schools hadn't been difficult, particularly when he posted so regularly about his failures on his blog. I might be his only reader. Tomorrow, he may have none.

"Don't look at me like that."

But I don't know what other way I can look at him. How does he want me to look? To smile? To nod understandingly? To give him reassurance in his mistakes? I certainly didn't receive any for mine.

"Maybe I should tell you a story." He drops the ice and kicks it aside. Livio flops onto the ground, still apparently unaware that he is sitting in a pile of hypothermia, and begins with a finer exercise in snowplay. Like a child building sandcastles. He forms oblong balls with his bare hands.

"I must have been nine years old. Hm...yes...nine. Nine years old. I never liked the winter. It wasn't the cold or the black ice. No, I didn't care about that. Feeling—it's just in the flesh. Bodies die—as we both know. It's what's around us that lives on. Call it an aura, an essence. I've always called it the Satium—the way we all satiate the empty vacuum of existence.

"The reason I didn't like winter was because it covered up the world. It was a symptom of that vacuum. Snow and ice and death. There's enough of that around. That's why I was always driven—always felt it was part of some sort of innate purpose in me—to build that aura back up. That seems almost ironic right now.

"My family differed in how that was meant to be. My mother thought I ought to go out and play, have fun, make friends—to submit this childlike joy to the world. I agreed with my father that that was a waste. There are things worth doing to build and grow that aren't so base.

"No—my purpose was to develop something. I didn't understand what that meant at nine years old, but my father did. He was always developing. Taking things and making them grow stronger—don't laugh!—he came from nothing and he created everything. Just because he was smart enough not to take it with him doesn't mean he didn't accomplish greatness.

"It took a long time for me to understand what he meant. There was a world underlying mine that I never knew about, not until today. He couldn't tell me. He knew I wasn't ready. My earliest warnings were lost on me. But I understand, now, how and why. It was a shock, but it shouldn't have been. I remember the furtive phone calls, the locked cellar doors, the trunks he transported back and forth in the dead of night, never seeing my silhouette watching him from the upstairs windows.

"I suspect, now, that I didn't understand because I never tried to. Maybe because I knew that to understand would have meant to acknowledge. And to acknowledge would have meant to be complicit. And to be complicit would have meant that everything would change.

"I had these dreams of joy being thrust upon me by my mother. She'd painted this holy picture of my future, with a wife and kids and a dog named Salter and a house by the lake in the heart of the hills. That would all be gone so quickly, just like she was. I never had a chance to say goodbye. My father made sure of that. The Satium only survives when it receives, and those awful emotions—sadness, anger, despair—they're like the cold. They take away.

"Don't make that face—there's a difference between sadness and despair. Sadness is a fleeting emotion. It comes and it goes. It lurks beneath the surface like all the other emotions, waiting for its turn. Despair is a poison that seeps through your brain and kills a little bit of your potential each moment it survives. There is only so high one can climb. Despair chops that ladder back to Earth until the only way to keep from falling any further is to hang yourself there.

"So, I never got to go to the funeral, even see the gravesite. First time I saw it was today, next to my father's. It looked unloved. There was a time I'd've thought that was a bad thing, but now it makes complete sense. Love is powerful. It's the closest thing to the reverse of despair, something that can revive your potential. It's not possible to revive what's dead, but as close as you can come to it. That's why we don't waste love on the vacuum. It gives to the Satium.

"I've said a lot of words. Most of them probably don't mean a thing to you. None of them matter. I'm wasting my breath—stupid! Stupid!—don't look at me like that. I'll strike myself down, if I feel like it. You'd probably like that, wouldn't you?

"But as I was saying…" He takes a deep breath here and looks at me with hard, blue eyes. They look black in the night, a craggy sepulchre for light.

"When I was nine years old, I thought to build and grow was a literal instruction, like I could build something great, even increase my impression on the world by doubling myself. I had this—I don't like to call it an attraction, that feels base. Call it a longing for the humanesque. Things that were not human but that were, for all intents and purposes, more human than we, ourselves.

"Frankenstein's monster. The ultimate humanesque creation. Frosty the Snowman.

"Yes, silly though it may seem, I loved a good snowman. Adored them, really. A snowman, to me, was the closest the average person could come to the holy creation. I wasn't allowed to build them, though. Maybe in part because I still didn't understand the true meaning of my father's demands. Maybe just because he couldn't stand my mother.

"She always told me, 'It's not a snow*man*...' she had that accent—that was a good impression, really. Kind of deep and growling, like a man, but in this petite body. Like a gremlin. A little, Germanic gremlin. 'It's not a snow*man*, Little Livvy'—she had this penchant for utterly asinine nicknames—'It's not a snow-*man*, Little Livvy, it is a snow-*friend*.'

"I can see it on your face even now, even when you know you don't want to laugh—you're laughing. You know how stupid it sounds. Snow*person*, okay. Pseudo-progressive cant designed to make people feel like they're making a difference when all they're doing is quibbling over meaningless symbols they, themselves, assigned undesirable meanings to. But at least it would be a normal evolution of language. Like mailperson or ombudsperson. Absurd in the illusion provided to the speaker. Forgotten the moment they're spoken.

"But snow-*friend*. What sort of a mentally deficient child would you need to be to stoop to such a ridiculous moniker? No, it's no more a person than it is a friend. But at least a person is just that. A friend—much like the imaginary friend, a snow-friend is a pathetic surrogate for the loneliest of scum.

"It was for that very reason my father banned me from ever making a 'snow-*friend*.' I respect him all the more for that now. More and more with each passing year. Then, I thought it was a punishment. I had no means of knowing that my mother was a simpleton, selected for breeding and child-rearing, beloved for her hips, not her heart. Then, I merely believed that my father wanted me to fail. He'd told me to grow and build and then taken away the manner in which to do so.

"So, would you imagine my surprise that eerie December morning when I came downstairs for breakfast and discovered my father in the backyard…allow me to set the scene."

Livio packs a lump of snow onto the structure he's building and massages it into place with care. He's been so lost in his story, he's equally lost time. I hope this will continue for a while. There's no telling what good it will do, but it can't do any worse.

The story flickers behind his craggy eyes.

"The sun was bright against the snow. It must have been nearly eleven. I always slept late in those days, in part because I could, in part because I didn't know what to do with myself. But one thing I always enjoyed was waking up to those violently bright days. I call them violent because that was how the sun felt, slapping against my eyes, cutting into me, carving away at my vision. That was the way to start a morning, being slapped straight into the brutality of reality.

"It had snowed the previous night, something wild. The wind had screeched and hollered and, I would've sworn, a few times, it had whispered. A screaming type of whisper, oozing beneath the cracks in my window, saying, 'Please help me! God help me!'

"By morning, the trees were bent and threatening to crack, to fall smack into the roof of the house and crush us in our beds. There were piles of snow as high as the windows. Cars were lost and not worth retrieving. It was a cold and barren desert of snow, and we were all isolated in its emptiness.

"Normally, my father would have been at the table on a weekend, reading the newspaper until nearly one in the afternoon. I suspect he was looking for something. He had friends at the press who would leave him messages, I only lately discovered. They were hidden, you see.

"On this morning, however, he was nowhere to be found for the longest time. Mother was still in bed with one of her 'headaches,' and I was inclined to eat a bag of chips for breakfast. But God forbid I get caught. I needed to be sure my father was out of the house. And that was when I found him in the backyard, gazing at the most humanesque snowman I'd ever seen.

"My father building a snowman? It couldn't have been. In fact, it must not have been. I stepped out of the house in just my bare feet—I think I lost some feeling that day. No matter. It's of no use to me. My father didn't notice or care, anyway. He was as astonished as I was.

"'Livio,' he said, 'did you build this…thing?'

"'Of course not,' I replied. 'I'm not allowed.'

"We both stared in wonder, so lost in curiosity that my father didn't notice me reach forward to touch the glinting, shining figure. I was like a magpie that morning. I needed to touch it because it shone and glowed and seemed like the most glorious thing in the universe. Even its shadow seemed bright.

"I'd barely touched the stomach when a clump of snow fell away, like an avalanche, cascading down onto my face and scarring me. You can still see one of the scars here, from where the ice did its damage. No? Well, I suppose it's dark, isn't it? It always gets dark early in the winter. You could almost believe it's after midnight, but it's only nine.

"My father probably wished it had been dark that morning. He tried to stop me, the moment he noticed, but it was far too late.

"I looked up, blinking blood from my eye, but hardly felt the pain. How could I when I was staring at the oblong nose and jagged face of a dead man? I crabwalked back and got one last look before my father blocked my sight. His eyes were closed. His face was blue. There was a sheen of white around his face that wasn't just from blood loss. He was a frozen man, entirely.

"My father, of course, immediately sent me inside while he called for help. My first thought was to run for my mother. Instead, my legs sat me at the kitchen table, too stunned to move or run or even call out.

"It felt like an age before my father returned. He told me that the ambulance had come and gone—I hadn't even heard it. I'd been aware of nothing. 'Will the man be all right?'

"'Of course, he will. He even told me to tell you thank you, for finding him.'

"That's why I forgot about the whole ordeal, I suppose. You might think that kind of traumatic discovery would stick with a person their entire life, but you must understand, the trauma was mitigated so calmly, so logically, that it seemed not to have occurred at all. Naturally, to find a dead body would have been horrifying. But the man was *not* dead—my father told me so. He was trapped, hidden. Had had a terrible accident befall him. But in the end, he was all right. More than fear, this renewed my faith in life and security, the knowledge that everything would turn out just fine. Maybe this was a man who had fulfilled the demands of the Satium. I needed only do the same.

"It wasn't until my father's funeral, just this morning, that I was reminded of the incident.

"In the snow, I've never known a burial to be rushed. When my mother died, we had to wait a month to put her in the ground. My father refused to cremate her. He said it was a waste of the world.

"My father though, despite his penniless exit from this world, had made certain of, shall we say, other types of gains. He had friends and influence. I've mentioned before that he had ties with the press. There were reasons to keep his remains from being…tampered with.

"I did very little. As the sole surviving relative, I'd expected a great deal of responsibility to befall me, but my father's lawyer—a mole-like little man named Pedersen, with pince-nez and a rump wider than any chair I've ever seen—Pedersen told me it had all been pre-arranged.

84

"Now, you can imagine my surprise at that. Not that I could complain, of course. I'm more broke than he was. My family's on the verge of losing the house. My children don't understand why their clothes have holes. We've convinced them that brunch is one of the two standard meals of the day.

"But for all my relief, it was a hell of a surprise. A forty-nine-year-old man, apparently without a dollar to his name, had pre-arranged his burial, his funeral, his will. It seemed improbable. Yet, there I was this morning, a mere viewer at the eternal passage of his father, watching him lowered into the ground by a sestet of tuxedoed men I'd never seen before, all in wraparound sunglasses and wearing a pin in the shape of a crow.

"As you can imagine, I felt impelled to learn more about my father's associates. I'd assumed them to be bankers. After all, my father had worked for Imperial Crown. I assumed the crow to be some sort of in-joke, a reference to the Crown. I suspected I may have been mistaken when the tall, balding fellow with the tattoo on his cheek and rings on all ten fingers grabbed the back of my neck and compressed me like an accordion. I'm sure I made an equally horrendous noise as I expanded again inside the car."

At this, he chortles and mimes the dying wail of a crushed accordion, a little more loudly than he intends. An icicle shakes perilously above his head. A part of me wills it to shuttle straight through the top of his skull and to paint his auburn hair sanguine. He stands and steps forward a moment later, murdering my dream.

"I won't bore you with the details of their little collective. Suffice it to say, my father's connections ran deeper than these snow dunes and thicker than the mud below. You don't retire from their brand of business, you understand. My father didn't. He planned to step away. Instead, he was buried quickly and quietly. I think they told me this to sound threatening, but it's difficult to perturb a man with so little left to lose. My wife plans to leave me and take the children. But I assume, in your investigations, you've probably long ago discovered that. I believe his name is Pedro? The bartender with a millionaire father and a blank cheque for the world, once he's proven he can make it a year on his own?

"I know Pedro. He doesn't know that I know him, but that's all right. He won't have to know much in a few days.

"But I digress.

"One thing you must understand about these men whom my father once knew. They are always building, always striving for something greater. They never give in to despair. If they did, they wouldn't be able to carry out their mandates. My father would have been sent to a beach to live out his days in peaceful retirement. These are men who understand that, to build, we must sometimes take away. To grow, we need a foundation on which to stand. We must irrigate our roots, whether by water or by blood.

"My blood, naturally, would have been next. I was a loose end, a mistake, a potential threat. In fact, I had my head just inches from the blade—you can see the cut…no, we've been through this. Much too dark.

86

Anyway, you'll have to believe me. I haven't told you a lie yet and I have no reason to do so.

"As I was saying, the blade was slicing into my neck when a old man up above, presiding over their little chamber in a winged suit, called for them to halt. He had his back to us from his perch on high. I barely made out his profile and he never turned. But I can tell you this: he wore on his face a mask, resembling the face of a crow.

"It was he who reminded the others of what my father had told them. I'm a trustworthy sort. I'm safe. I would never speak a word to a soul. You see—my father didn't die because he was untrustworthy, but because he couldn't be allowed to live. His word was still golden in their circles. And if he vouched for me, I was approved.

"He reminded the men of the snowman. Of the body my father had hidden, hoping for a delay, hoping to keep his secret masked until the night, when he might remove it without suspicion.

"Never for a moment had I suspected. I'd forgotten entirely, as I've said. But it made sense now. The reason my father had wasted his energies on the wrong type of building, why he had built a snow-*friend*. I held my tongue, naturally, but my body went cold and numb at this discovery. I don't think I've felt a thing since.

"I was still in this state of absence when I discovered the face-tattooed fellow snapping his fingers in my face. His voice was low and gruff, much like my mother's. But without the hideous accent. 'Do we have a deal?' he asked me.

"I implored that he repeat the terms. You see, I was naturally prepared to agree to anything that would allow me to leave that little chamber with my life, but to keep myself living as long as possible, it seemed important to know what I was agreeing to.

"What he told me…is of little consequence for you. I've been sworn to secrecy and let's allow that to die with us this evening. Suffice it to say, my father had been involved in a certain business that would have ensnared him a certain financial comfort. There's very little required of me to complete the job. More a matter of not blowing everything up. And then I'll keep the house, keep the kids. As for the wife…we'll see how things go with Eloise and Pedro. I have other thoughts.

"It had all come together. In the death of my father, I had inherited his Satium. It was my time to build. And the best part was, to do it, I had to do *nothing*.

"And then came the one thing that could obliterate my prospects. The cruel tap-a-tap-tap on my door. A woman—a pretty woman, I'll admit, but one who could have been prettier if her face hadn't been so deranged by years of unbridled obsession. A woman with blonde hair, prematurely greying, hard eyes that had all the world's potential to be soft. But that's what despair will do to a body. It will kill that potential.

"Don't you see the way it killed your potential?"

Livio leans in close until I can smell the repugnant swirl of garlic and salami on his breath. He's close enough now that I can see the rot of his front tooth in the fading, distant orange of the streetlight. He's twenty-nine but he looks fifty. A reflection of his father. A boy trying futilely to build a man, and already on the brink of eternity.

He pulls away and piles together another clump of snow.

"There you were on my doorstep, speaking of ancient grievances. A father you'd loved and lost. A suspicion that you *claimed* no longer mattered. What did you expect? That I would confess to the crimes of my father? Well, in that, I suppose you were partly right. Yes, my dear woman—my cruel woman—it was my father's hand which led that of your father into the pits of Hell! Delivered courtesy of a snow-friend.

"But my father's work had only just begun, and I am his new messenger. I live in the aura that he cast and left behind. I am the spawn of his Satium, as my son shall be the spawn of mine. And much like my father, twenty years ago, I cannot—I *will* not—allow all that I've built to crumble beneath the weight of despair."

He turns his head to the side and finally I can see the cuts. A nick on his neck. A slice above his eye. In the shadows of the streetlight, his scars grow darker than the Devil's burnt fingernails.

Livio can't bring himself to look at me as he places the final ball of snow over my face and completes his snow-friend.

Defiance, in honour of his father.

I, now, am the humanesque beast he has created.

The last I hear—before my ears freeze away and the cold, empty air takes me into the ultimate vacuum—is a cry of excitement from a boy who does not yet know that he is lost.

"Daddy, Daddy! Can I play with the snow-friend?"

The Hampburg Crow

I.

THE HUNTER STOOD across the road from the Hampburg Estate, looking pointedly at the old house that rose like a crag against the night sky. There were no lights in the windows, but the Hunter knew they were awake. They would not sleep until the crow had returned. The deed had been done. He hadn't gotten there in time, although he'd tried. He'd waited and watched and searched the skies, but by the time he'd arrived, the blood had run too far to be stuffed back into the tattered human shell.

The Hunter's fingers clenched, his palms matted with the sweat of rage. What he wouldn't give to flood the home in that sweat and drown its inhabitants. He could never be certain what the Hamburgs knew, but they knew enough to stop it. They'd made their choice long ago and had only cultivated it since. They were untouchable now, forever protected by the crow and its kin.

A headlight flickered in the distance and pulled into a neighbour's driveway. The Hunter lifted his black overcoat up against his cheek, hiding his face from the night. It was a futile game. They knew he was there just as he knew that they watched through those thin upstairs curtains. A pregnant standoff. A battle of unspoken threats that no combatant would dare to act on. Not yet. Not without the star of the show present. And even then…

…now wasn't the time.

Something slapped against the wind, shrouded in the darkness above. A speck plummeted like a bullet toward the chimney, unafraid of the smoke that wafted in thick, grey clouds over the home.

The world was safe again, for the time being. But time is short, and Hell never sleeps.

The Hunter turned down the street, his footsteps weighted down by the thought of that poor boy, the thought of a thousand poor boys who would follow.

Somewhere in the house, something screeched.

II.

DETECTIVE CRAVEN ACKERSLEY butted out a cigarette with his shoe. He'd given up smoking three years earlier when the doctors had told him about the grey mass growing in his lung. A biopsy had found the mass to be benign, but the threat had been enough for Ack. He'd quietly quit cold turkey without telling anyone why. It wasn't fear, exactly, that drove his decision. But he hadn't liked the idea that he had no control over his fate, that his body was going to do to him what he had spent so many years doing to it. He still lit one up before he set foot on any crime scene, though. There was something peaceful about the smell of tobacco. It reminded him of the casino he'd practically grown up in, the bowling alleys where he'd won a little more than he'd claimed on his taxes, the back-alley meetings he'd arranged with perps before the floodlights flashed and the night descended into a gunfight.

Ack's partner, Anaïs Piers, was already in the tunnel, along with coroner Tina Li and a troop of low-level officers who were photographing the scene, swabbing for DNA, setting up lights, manning the caution tape. Ack scoffed. No point in caution tape out here on the edge of town. Even the sewage workers barely checked on these relics of a less sophisticated time. This morning's exception had been an unfortunate convenience. Teenagers had tried throwing parties out here back when the tunnels had first closed down. Drugs and alcohol and illicit sex, away from the prying eyes of parents. So isolated on the edge of the city limits that even the keenest, cruellest of cops didn't bother patrolling out here, not even for an easy charge to pad the stats. Those parties hadn't lasted long. The smell was rancid. The ground was wet and dirty. Funny, Ack thought, how a little fecal matter could turn off the dirtiest of gigs.

The smell of excrement and rotting leaves struck Ack like a wall of poison the moment he ducked under the caution tape, and he longed for another whiff of his dead cigarette. The air was heavy and humid in the tunnel. Breathing became work, worse still when you were trying not to breathe in the first place. Ack's jaw clenched further with each splash that oozed into his socks. The ridges by his eyes hardened.

Why the kid had come out here, they might never know. But why did ten-year-olds do anything? Curiosity, a rush, general stupidity…Ack tended toward the latter. He'd spent two years as a guard at a juvenile detention hall before getting accepted into the academy. He was just feeling the relief of being away from those snotty, Neanderthalic brats when the universe had had the sense of humour to assign him to a juvenile unit—because of his *experience*. It had taken him three years to get away from kids and into serious crimes. There was no homicide unit in Reamish. Big enough to have a juvenile-focus unit, but not to have separate units for homicides and serious crimes. Then again, how many homicides had there been since Ack had transferred eight years earlier? Six? And five of them had been solved with spousal confessions within forty-eight hours. Ack didn't like to think about the other.

He supposed it was inevitable that he'd end up dealing with kids again, even if they weren't doing much these days. He liked 'em better quiet, he'd always said. He didn't mean dead though. Dead made him angry. Dead was one more loss for the human race and one more win for the Devil.

Four in three days, though…

The kid in the park didn't count. She'd just frozen after her mother'd kicked it in the road. Open and shut. Nature had even done the morgue's work for them.

The other two before this afternoon hadn't been quite so easy. Violently mutilated, organs missing. A random, haphazard splatter-job. But there was method to it, consistency, a clear target. An unstable hand that knew what it wanted to do but didn't have the where-withal to do well. Ack still hadn't seen the latest body, but when the sewage worker had called it in, his voice had been hollow and airy, his mind a million miles away and trying to stay there. Ack had no doubt about what he was about to see.

His suspicions were only confirmed by the look on Piers' face as she watched him trek through the sludge. She looked sick, greener than the muck beneath their feet. She had been in the business longer than he had. She'd been involved in some of the most difficult operations the unit had ever seen while Ack was still wasting away with a group of future felons. Piers had killed a man to save a family. Ack had never killed a man, although there had been plenty he'd wanted to.

Still, Piers had her limits, and she had never done well with corpses. "I knew I wanted to be a cop," she'd told him, unasked and unprovoked, on one of their first cases together, "when I watched all those great detective shows from the '90s. I guess I kinda expected they'd all be like that. Naïve, I know, but those shows all looked so real at the time. It was like I thought the whole world existed before the water-shed." Ack hadn't responded—he'd never been one for TV. He'd known he wanted to be a cop when he'd seen a photo of one of Ed Gein's trophies.

"Same," Ack said now. It wasn't a question.

Piers nodded.

She'd made a good call keeping her mouth shut. Ack had regretted speaking the moment the poison aroma had scalded a layer off his tongue.

He took a straight line for the body, nearly walking through a young, uniformed officer who apologized even though Ack had walked into her. Ack and his six-foot-five, muscular frame barely noticed.

His face didn't change as he stared down at the body. Li looked more disgusted about that than she did about the sight of the corpse.

It could have been any of the three children they'd discovered so far. Soaked in blood, with splatters across the walls and drifting away in the sewage. The boy's face was torn to shreds. His body had fared much worse. There was a chasm dug out of the centre of his chest. Even in the low light of the lamps that had been hung around the tunnel, it was clear that the chest had been hollowed out.

"Same."

Li sighed and looked away, but he knew she'd rolled her eyes. "Sometimes, Ack…I know it's a coping mechanism or whatever…"

Ack scoffed. "I feel nothing."

"It's cold."

"It's life."

"It's death, actually."

"What's the difference?"

Tina Li shook her head. "Whatever, Ack. You wanna hear the facts or do you think all living things look like this?"

"Let me guess. Chest wound came first. Took the lungs, then the rest of the organs, and finally the heart. Didn't leave a bit of organ behind."

"Lucky guess."

"Educated guess." He grimaced. "As for the face…"

"Defensive wounds."

"You telling me the kid tried to fight back with his face?"

Li stepped closer to where the body was crumpled against the tunnel wall. She crossed herself as she crouched, as she did every time she neared a body, whether it was for the first time or the last. "You see these cuts?" She indicated the slashes that ran up and down the boy's cheeks, the ones that had cleaved his face in two.

"Not at all. Looks happy and healthy."

She glared at him. He didn't blink. "Anyway, what I was *going* to say was: these cuts start at the bottom and rise up. Looks like the kid tried to get up or move and whatever blade or tool this guy was using…" She mimed an upward swipe. "…straight through the flesh."

"Still no idea on the weapon?"

Li shook her head. "Nothing I've ever seen. Lab's still running the results from the last two, but everything I'm seeing here suggests we're looking at the same type of tool, whatever it is."

Ack sighed. He turned toward Piers.

"Good to see you too," Li huffed as he walked away. She whispered something else but Ack chose to ignore it.

"Same."

"Same."

"I'm getting annoyed."

Piers drummed her fingers against her crossed arms. "Not exactly the word I was going to use, but sure. Annoyed. Whatever."

"Anything?"

She shook her head. "They're still swabbing but nothing's turned up yet. Same as the others. No footprints, no DNA."

"Need to check upstream." Ack jabbed a thumb toward the depths of the tunnel.

Piers sighed. "Not sure what good it'd do. Not like they monitor currents in abandoned sewage tunnels."

"Has to be something," Ack grunted. "People don't just fly in and commit a murder without touching the ground." He looked down. "Even we've left shoeprints in this gunk."

Piers was still shaking her head. He realized that she'd been shaking it since the moment he'd stopped next to her. "Nothing when they got in here. I've seen the pictures. Guy either wiped them away or doesn't have feet."

"Isn't going to have feet when we're done with 'em."

Piers flinched.

"Fine. When *I'm* done with 'em."

"Can we get out of here?"

Ack was already headed for the caution tape.

"I don't like it, Ack," Piers said when they'd finally gotten away from the acrid must of the tunnel.

Ack took a deep breath of fresh air and closed his eyes. His shoulders tensed. He kicked out at the first thing he saw: a fallen black feather, sticking straight up from the mud. It bounced right back into place. He kicked it again for good measure. It popped back. He stomped on it and left his foot there. Ack pinched the bridge of his nose. "Three murdered kids in three days. We've got twenty-four hours at most."

"This is all your fault!"

Ack released his nose and turned to Piers, an incredulous look on his face. But she wasn't looking at him. In fact, she hadn't spoken at all.

Ack followed her gaze to the bluffs above, towering beside the lake. A woman was standing on the precarious peninsula of snow that crested the edge of the bluffs.

"I told ya's. I told ya's and ya didn't listen!"

"Imelda…" Piers began, starting for the uncleared, icy path that led to the peak.

But Imelda McGovern had no interest in listening. Ack could see the tears in her eyes from twenty feet below, glistening in the sharp glow of the winter sun. Her voice cracked, "I told ya's and ya wouldn't listen…"

"Imelda," Piers said as softly as she could without losing a tone of firm authority. "This is a crime scene. You shouldn't be here." She paused and, when there was no reaction, she added, "It's not safe."

"It ain't been safe in weeks." Imelda swatted Piers away as the detective came close behind her. Piers slipped on the ice but caught herself before she could fall. Ack stared up at the scene impassively. "I told ya's…"

"Imelda, we have no reason to believe this has any connection with your cat…" Piers said, but she couldn't keep uncertainty from her tone.

"Cloyton. Cloyton the Cat had a name, gawdunnit!"

"Imelda…it's time to go home. Your grandkids are probably worried…"

"Don't tell me none about my grandkids. Ya's all don't know a thing about nothin'. Ain't never solved a thing worth a damn and ya's goin' on tellin' me what's what! Rot in Hell, coppers. Rot in Hell." She took her face in both hands and wept, a fading old woman withering in the cold.

Piers returned to Ack, a worried grimace on her face. "We need to get her home," she whispered. "Away from here."

"The state ruled her competent."

"You and I both know that's a load of B.S. If she and Judge Randal hadn't gone to school together…"

"The state ruled her competent. She's on her own."

Ack started up the hill toward the road.

Piers took one last look back at Imelda, now wailing on her knees at the edge of the bluffs. Then, she followed her partner.

III.

ACK DRUMMED THE fingers of his right hand against the steering wheel. His left elbow was propped against the window, holding his face up. He stared with an empty, bored expression at the front door of the small, lower-middle-class house in front of him. It was the most boring house he'd ever seen. The walls were painted white. There was one door and one window and one floor. Even the car was boring. A rusty green sedan that had been old when the family had bought it twenty years earlier.

This was the worst bit: telling the family.

That was why Ack refused to take part.

And Piers approved of that decision very much. He lacked what she called "bedside manner." He argued that it wasn't a bedside.

It was the crying that Ack couldn't stand. The sadness was understandable, predictable, even boring. He could handle a few sighs, could even force his mouth to fake a gentle smile as the family reminisced about the good times, although his eyes could never match his lips. When it came to tears and hugs and chest-pounding cries of "Why couldn't it have been me instead?!"—that was when Ack checked out.

100

Apparently, it wasn't "respectful" to say, "Have a good day," and walk away while a grieving mother was in the midst of a weeping fit. Ack begged to differ.

"I'm giving them their space during this…trying time," he'd said, as though reading from a textbook on human emotions written by an author he didn't particularly approve of.

Piers had responded with a cold glare.

Ack drummed louder and faster, as though speeding up the music would speed up the scene. He'd been staring at that door for…he checked his watch…three whole minutes. That couldn't be right. His watch had to have stopped. The second hand appeared to freeze. Then, it continued.

Ack checked his phone to see if Li had gotten back to them with any results. It was a little game he played with himself any time he wanted to be frustrated, annoyed, or both at the same time. He was unsurprised to find nothing from Li or any of the albatrosses at the lab—he called them all albatrosses for the coats they wore that looked like wings but that didn't seem to get them anywhere with any sort of reasonable human speed.

He did discover a text from an unknown number.

Another scam. Another "We've sent the money *wink*". Ack had had a friend who'd fallen for one of those scams once. He hadn't remained a friend much longer.

He was about to delete the text when two words caught his eye.

"Hampburg crow"

He paused.

101

"The Hampburg crow has returned. He will kill again."

Ack knew the stories. Everyone knew the stories. They were old wives' tales, made up horrors to keep kids on the straight and narrow, to keep them out of the types of centres that Ack used to patrol or the ones Li frequented in the basement. They were the types of stories he'd grown out of believing in consciously at six years old and subconsciously at fourteen. The last alleged "attack" of the Hampburg crow had occurred thirty-two years ago, when he'd been only two years old. It was stupid—a ridiculous text from an anonymous number. But still…

He was staring at the text when he heard the car door close. Piers slid in beside him.

"You would've liked that one," she said with a hint of anger in her tone. "She didn't cry once."

"I heard her screaming through the walls with the doors closed," Ack replied, but his voice was far away, with his mind.

"What're you looking at?"

He blinked and put the phone down. Then, he blinked some more. "What do you know about the Hampburg crow?"

Piers frowned, "What the *hell* are you on about?"

"The Hampburg crow. The attacks back in the early-'90s."

"I was a child."

"Older than me."

"Thanks for reminding me. Two years. See how *your* bones ache when you get to thirty-six."

"I'm being serious right now."

"When are you not?"

102

"Anaïs." He looked up sharply and she hesitated with her mouth slightly open.

"I don't know much. Just the same stories all the kids hear. What's the old nursery rhyme? *Go out alone and the crow will get you/Better stay home, or the crow will get you/He'll feed off your groans, and he'll tear you apart/If the Hampburg crow gets you, he'll eat out your...*" She stopped, a look of shock crossing her face.

"*Heart,*" Ack finished.

"It's a stupid children's story."

"I know. But…" He turned his phone to face her. She ignored the lewd lockscreen image of a nude woman riding a horse and read the message to herself three times. "Did anyone ever look into those old stories about the crow?"

"The murders were never solved; I know that."

"Get on the phone to Bircham. Have him pull the old files." Ack turned the key and was halfway down the driveway before Piers could get her seatbelt on.

"Where are we going?"

"I think we'd better pay a visit to Lo and Hiram Hampburg."

IV.

THE HAMPBURG ESTATE towered above the surrounding houses by two storeys without counting the spires that rose from each corner of the roof. Windows were scattered across the façade at apparently random intervals, each taking the form of a tall arch. Each was covered with a red curtain. The front door, as well, rounded into an arch and was divided into two separate doors, although only one had a handle. The handle was of black metal and curved like a doorknocker. In lieu of a lawn, the home was fronted with a patch of bare dirt that had been dug out several inches below the asphalt pathway that led from the sidewalk to the door. There was no space for a car. The Hampburgs' chauffeur lived nearby and was on call at all hours to transport the couple, who rarely left their home.

Ack started for the door but Piers stopped on the sidewalk.

"What're you waiting for?" He turned, hands clenched.

"You don't feel that?"

"All I feel is winter. Don't feel like standing around in it."

She frowned. "You don't feel that…I don't know how to describe it. Heaviness? Like your whole mind's being hitched up to anvils?"

Ack blinked. "What the hell are you talking about?" He didn't want to admit that he felt it too, a darkness encroaching on the corners of his brain, a lethargy grasping at his body, the sense of hands dragging him into the ground, pulling harder with each passing step. He didn't want to admit it because it was impossible, a trick of the mind. Ack was here for facts.

He turned and Piers followed slowly, each step seeming to echo in her ears. The sound only became worse as Ack pounded on the door. None of the sounds fully disappeared. They stayed and swirled in a cacophony of bangs and creaks.

The door cracked open, just a sliver, exposing a long streak of blackness within. The door screeched on its hinges, opening inch by inch, until Ack and Piers found themselves face-to-face with a dour-looking man whose countenance remained forever immovable. He was well over eighty, but he had the stature and presence of a man thirty years younger.

"Can I help you?" asked Hiram Hampburg in a low, slow voice. *A heavy voice*, Piers thought, his words being dragged down like her mind had been.

"Mr. Hampburg," Ack began, standing up taller to maintain a slight height advantage over the other man. "I'm Detective Ackersley and this is Detective Piers from the Reamish Serious Crimes Unit…"

"I'm aware of who you are. Why are you here?"

"We've been investigating a series of murders and would like to ask you a few questions."

Hiram Hampburg stood still a moment, assessing him. The door creaked open another few inches. Then, the man turned and stepped further into the house. Ack glanced to Piers. She shrugged.

"Are you coming?" came a voice, echoing from deep within the house.

Ack started in, pushing at the door. He suddenly understood why it had taken the elderly man so long to open up. It was the heaviest door Ack had come across. Just moving it a few inches to slip his large frame through left his arm sore. Once inside, he stopped to allow Piers to pass so that he could close the door behind them. She would go no further. Not until Ack had finished with the door and had taken the lead.

"I don't like this," she whispered. Piers had always trusted her gut. It had kept her safe from a sniper during an undercover drug bust. It had told her to run from that abandoned shack behind the trainyard a minute before the place blew to bits. When she'd infiltrated the dogfight operation during the carpet store boom, it had told her that that growl wasn't coming from a cage.

Even then, she had only felt a twinge of uncertainty in each case. Right now, her gut was turning inside out and backward. It wasn't the same type of immediate danger she'd felt then. This was something creeping, lying in wait, infiltrating the pores in preparation for a long-term attack.

"It's just a few questions," said Ack.

They passed through the front hall, past a suit of armour that was covered in a thick layer of dust, a ticking grandfather clock that was off by two and a half hours, and a painting of a gendarme carrying a musket fitted with a bayonet. The lighting was poor, with only a few covered wall lamps glowing a dull yellow. The floorboards felt oddly thin. Piers stepped lightly. Ack ignored the feeling.

They followed the hall to a large living room that took up the bulk of the first floor. The space in the heart of the room was sparsely adorned, but the walls were cluttered. Above the fireplace, there was a painting of Hiram and Lola Hampburg. She sat, wearing a bulky blue dress, and he stood with one hand on her shoulder. They both wore vacant expressions, staring straight forward and through the viewer. The background of the painting was pure burgundy, aside from the presence of a simplistic table with an empty

106

birdcage on top. The side walls displayed a variety of small paintings and placards, some awards for hunting or croquet, others bearing the names of high-class societies along with years. Ack scanned a few of the names and recognized none of them. The furniture in the room consisted of two aquamarine couches forming an ell before the fireplace, a long oak table with a candelabra at its centre, and a smaller circular table in the corner of the room. This was topped with a covered bell. Piers looked to Ack with a grimace. They both knew what was below that cover.

Lola Hampburg sat on one of the couches, facing the wall where the covered bell was. She wore the same blue dress as she did in the painting, but her hair had turned from jet black to bright white. She held her hands clasped in her lap and stared straight ahead, without anything to occupy her. She seemed to be waiting, as though she had expected company at any moment. Hiram Hampburg stood in the centre of the room on a worn oriental rug, with his arms at his sides. The lighting was nominally better in this room than it had been in the hall, but it still cast dark shadows across their host's face, making him appear more his age.

"Mr. Hampburg." Ack nodded to him, then turned to his wife. "Mrs. Hampburg."

"I've seen you in the newspaper," Lola Hampburg said without turning her head. "Detectives Ackersley and Piers. Yes. I remember. That awful murder of that girl without a name."

She paused and Piers looked to Ack, uncomfortable.

"It never was solved, was it?" Lola Hampburg finished, and now she turned to look at them. Her eyes were a deep blue and caught the full brunt of the low light. Her jaw was tight. Though she spoke softly, almost weakly, with a shake in her voice, those eyes were meant to challenge them. She remained in place, never taking her eyes off Ack's. He stared right back. Piers looked away. Neither detective responded to Lola Hampburg's remark. Neither cared to remember.

"We have some questions…" Ack started.

Hiram Hampburg cut him off. "Regarding the recent string of child murders."

"We never said…"

"It's obvious." Something sharp flickered in his look. "Please don't waste our time. We're busy people."

Piers looked around the room, breathed in the stale, dead atmosphere. She couldn't fathom what two octogenarians had to do so urgently. "You sound like you're familiar with the details of the case. We'll start with the basics. Were you personally familiar with any of the victims."

"No," replied Hiram.

"Indeed. No," Lola said.

"Can you think of any reason why someone would want to hurt the children of this town, or anyone who would?"

They repeated their previous answers with the same tone and brevity.

"Have you witnessed…?"

Ack held up a hand to stay his partner, his eyes still locked on Lola Hampburg's. He pointed to the covered bell on the small table. "What's under there?"

For the first time since they'd arrived, Hiram Hampburg's face changed. A small smile crept onto the corners of his lips. "Thank you, Detective Ackersley, for not wasting any more of our time. In return, we'll not waste yours. You see, Lo, as we suspected. The detectives of our little town have fallen victim to the pull of fairy stories."

Hiram Hampburg strode across the room and stood beside the covered bell, looking down at it. "The Hampburg crow. I remember the first time I heard the term. It must have been sixty years ago. It started with the mayor, if I'm not mistaken. Alburius Chattenby. A man of limited intellect but grand pomposity. He had it in for us—that's how the stories started. But I'm sure you already knew that." He looked up at Piers. She avoided eye contact. Ack glared, but Hiram wouldn't face him.

That much they had known. Bircham had pulled the files and called them along their route. What he'd told them was uninspiring.

"This feels like a waste of time," Piers had said.

Ack had said nothing, had kept on driving. Something about that text had him convinced, but he couldn't say why. The feeling of this house only confirmed his suspicions.

The details on the Hampburg crow were consistent with the various poems that had been whispered over the years. Legends of a crow that lived in the Hampburg home, released at nights every few decades to wreak havoc on the citizens of Reamish, leaving a trail of animal and human bodies in its wake. The

109

home had been searched thirty-two years earlier when a concerned citizen claimed to have seen the bird fly from the crime scene back to the house, but no crow had been discovered. That story later turned out to be a false report. Ack fought to ignore that the text might be the same.

"That's what you expect to see here, isn't it? Our evil little crow?" Hiram smirked. He pinched the cloth between two fingers and whipped it off the bell with a flourish.

Beneath was the bird cage they had expected, but not the bird. Instead of a crow, black and dreary, they gazed upon the majestic rainbow of a macaw, perched on a railing within its prison. The bird turned to the visitors and tilted its head.

"Come forward, come forward." Hiram beckoned the detectives. Piers stepped toward the cage on instinct. Ack remained rooted to the spot.

"He's quite friendly. Come say 'hi.'"

"What's his name?" Piers leaned close to the bird, studying the pattern of green, yellow, blue, and red that painted its wings in swirls and splashes.

"He doesn't have one," replied Lola from her place on the couch. "He never has."

Piers bent lower, studying the bird's claws and finding nothing out of the ordinary. Ack's eyes fixed on its face. "I want to get a mould of that bird's beak."

Hiram smiled. "When you produce a warrant, we'll be most happy to comply. Until then, if there's no reason to suspect us of wrongdoing beyond the tales of children and their mothers…"

Ack strode forward, his heavy steps echoing off the hollow floor. He produced his phone and stuffed the text in Hiram's face. "I'd call that more than a children's story."

Hiram removed his glasses from his pocket and deliberately took his time in affixing them to his nose. His eyes flicked up at Ack, unimpressed. "I would consider that precisely the kind of story to which I referred." His cold grin remained locked in place.

Ack didn't react. In fact, he'd accomplished precisely what he'd wanted. With his phone now in hand, he easily snapped two quick photographs of the bird before sliding it back into his pocket.

"If you have nothing more to tell us," Ack said, "we'll be pursuing our warrant. We'll be in contact shortly."

Piers rose back up and glanced from the bird to each Hampburg in turn. "Thank you for your time…"

"You may show yourselves out. It's such an effort to walk in one's old age," Hiram Hampburg said with a gesture to the door. Ack took one final hard look at his host before turning toward the exit. Piers rushed to follow. Hiram called after them as they disappeared down the hall, "Feel free to look around. I'm sure you'll find nothing."

Ack walked on without stopping. He had what he'd come for and had no interest in the dust. Piers wouldn't have stopped even if there had been a rotting corpse hanging from the ceiling. She needed to get out.

Although, something deep in her gut told her that she could leave this house, but that it would never truly leave her.

111

V.

THE BODY HAD been cleared away, but the dent had frozen in the snow, a snow angel of death. A worthless, bloodless death. It didn't matter to the Hunter. A part of him stood in reverence by the indentation, saying a silent prayer for the eviscerated soul. It had not been used but it would not find peace. This, he could feel. Something flickered against the black of the night and was gone. The time to mourn had passed.

The Hunter held the powder in one hand, a mixture of his own creation. It had worked once before, in a lifetime that no longer existed. The birds had grown stronger.

That wasn't right.

The power beneath them had grown stronger.

The birds themselves were little more than a vessel. Really, they weren't birds at all.

The Hunter patrolled past the park and onto the streets. There was no promise that tonight would be the night. It could be tomorrow; it could be in the day; it could have happened already. In the night, he could watch without being watched. He'd been a suspect before. There were times he blamed himself, wished he'd been taken before he could fail again. But each day in captivity would be another win for death.

He had prowled in the day with the subtlety of a dog in kitty Hell. There were times he passed for a usual man, on big city streets that took all kinds, where money-mongers, whores, and children on crack coexisted with mutual understanding. These parts were much too quiet for a man like him. These people hid their secrets, buried them in snowmen, sequestered them to closed roads.

His face was a normal face. Plain, blank, forgettable. His height was average, his weight a little low but unspectacularly so. He dressed as close to a standard man as he could, in a coat and pants, although he felt very little of the cold. What he could not hide was the way he shook, the way his head snapped from side to side in constant search. The Hunter couldn't stop hunting. It was not in his nature or permitted by his assignment.

The crow could have been anywhere.

During the day, parents had pulled their children across roads to avoid the unusual man. Dogs had barked at him as terrified owners rushed to pass. An older woman had held her cane in defense across her body. Surely, the crow knew he was there, had watched him from a faraway perch, waiting for its moment, when no one was looking.

Perhaps the crow had read the clouds. Tonight, there were hundreds, matted into a thick paste across the sky. There was supposed to be a nearly full moon to illuminate every secret. Instead, the Hunter found black against black as he searched for black. The streetlamps were much too low. The crow flew as near as he could to the Heavens without being smote. Taunting.

The clouds grew darker with the night and showed no signs of passing. Thicker, angular clouds replaced the weak putty across the sky. They portended a winter storm.

The night had become too warm. The Hunter felt little, but he could tell that something wasn't right. The air was heavy. These were not snow clouds.

A bolt of lightning cleaved the sky in two.

A flicker of black descended rapidly in the heart of the bolt.

A high scream rose against the night air.

It was swallowed in the boom of thunder, which rocked the windowpanes across the entire street.

A light flicked on in a window. When the woman within looked to the street where the Hunter had so recently stood, she found nothing but an empty road and the sharp fall of freezing rain.

The Hunter sprinted around street signs. He didn't look as he crossed roads. He heard no traffic. His foot slipped on the ice. His body was weighted down with the icy rain. Still, he'd crossed six blocks in just minutes.

He knew that he would be too late. He still had to try.

The Hunter slowed as he approached the dark mound in the heart of the street. He stood beneath a flickering streetlight and watched the rain sweep blood across the asphalt in currents. The drains dripped red.

A van skidded to a halt behind him. The driver leaned on his horn.

The Hunter didn't acknowledge anything but the young boy who had been reduced to little more than a pile of shredded skin.

The crow was long gone.

The Hunter cursed himself. He cursed the universe for allowing such a damned thing to occur, such a damned thing to survive.

He had played this safely for too long. There was no more time for cautious observation.

It was time for him to tackle the beast at the source.

VI.

PIERS PULLED HER coat tightly around herself but it was no good, not in a storm this violent. "Waterproof" had been something of an overstatement. Droplets of ice had frozen to the hairs on her arms. She tried to ignore them, resisted every human urge to shiver. She wasn't supposed to show weakness. People expected it of her. They didn't see a hardened police detective at the best of times. They saw a young woman who was out of her depths. There were days she wished she had grey hair, wrinkles, and a broken nose to prove her worth. She'd never looked her age. At twenty-five she'd been called a teenager. At thirty-six, she'd finally started to look like she'd reached her mid-twenties. There had been a time she'd tried to age herself. She'd cut her hair short and worn exclusively grey. When one-too-many men had told her she looked like a child playing dress-up in Daddy's finest, she'd given up the ruse. She would speak with her actions.

That became harder as the storm increased.

The road was slick with black ice, but she couldn't even see the road. White pellets had joined in with the rain to form a dirty, spiralling wall. Piers couldn't trust that she was still in the section of street that had been taped off. She couldn't trust that cars could see the tape. She would have stepped onto the corpse if an arm hadn't cut across her chest just in time.

"You should be wearing a coat," she screamed up at Ack.

He didn't bother looking over.

If he hadn't just swung a muscular biceps in her way, she might have thought he'd frozen like that, a statue in the night.

Piers turned to the ground where two officers held umbrellas over Li, who crouched beside the victim. There was no doubt in Piers' mind that they were dealing with a victim. She thought of Ack's cold "Same" comment from the previous scene and a perverse smile cracked across her face. She was thankful that it was lost in the night.

Li turned up to them, her face a blur in the darkness, but her expression clear from the sigh in her tone. "I think you two could probably give yourselves the rundown by memory at this point."

"How long?" Ack asked.

"Lotta rain. Hard to say for sure."

He grunted and turned to survey the scene, squinting as though he could see anything at all.

"What're you thinking?" Piers pulled her coat tighter, until she'd almost cut off her breathing.

"Anonymous tip. Said he hadn't seen it but knew it had just happened."

"You think it might be the killer called it in?"

Ack pulled out his phone and shielded it from the rain. He flicked through it, his face growing darker as he struggled against the drops that marred his screen.

Finally, he showed Piers the email he'd been looking for.

The tip had come from a fake number. Gavvy, down at the station, was still trying to trace it back to a name.

Piers shook her head. "That number supposed to mean anything to me?"

Ack flipped open his texts by way of response. There was the same number. The tip they'd received regarding the Hampburgs.

"You think this guy's trying to throw us off his scent?"

"I think no human did that to that kid."

Piers gritted her teeth and turned to face the mess behind them. For the first time, she was grateful for the wall of water blocking her vision.

"He knows something," Ack said.

"There's not a lot of evidence…"

"That macaw."

"Looked pretty docile to me. It's a starting point, but until we get a warrant…"

"We don't need a warrant." Ack turned back to Li and shoved his phone in her face. She instinctively pulled away.

"The hell, Ack?"

"The beak." He indicated the furtive picture of the macaw he'd taken earlier that day. He traced down the curve of the yellow beak, resting his finger at the pointed black tip. "Could that do this?" He jutted his chin toward the mangled body.

Li squinted in the darkness, moving closer to the phone. She said nothing. Ack's body tensed. Rain

117

dripped across his eyelids. He'd stopped feeling the cold a long time ago. Sometimes, it felt like years.

Finally, Li shook her head. "I can't say for sure, but I doubt it. The amount of force needed—I don't even think that bird's neck would bend far enough to get the momentum. But even if it did, you see how thin the point is? These gashes are too thick."

Ack glared in silence.

"Whaddaya want me to say?" Her tone turned harsh. "Yeah, that's the beak that did it. Woo-hoo! We got our guy. Hope you can get cuffs on that thing! Stuff it up your ass, Ack." She turned back to her crime scene and brushed him away with one hand. "Get me a model of the beak and I'll give it a test. But if you ask me, I think you're reaching."

"I'll do the policing."

"Then, do it. I have testing to get back to before the rest of this kid becomes rat food."

Piers reappeared at his side, her hood down past her eyes. "You're not going to get a warrant off that photo, you know that."

Ack grunted. "I'll find a way." He started toward his car.

Piers followed behind as quickly as she could without slipping. Ack had no apparent fear of the ice.

"If you get suspended again, I swear to God…"

He swung around so sharply that Piers nearly barrelled into his chest. He took a slow, heavy breath. "Don't mention that again."

Piers held her ground. There had been a time when she might have given way, let him go without further incident. She had never been scared of him, not the way her colleagues had. His first partner had

118

requested a transfer. His second had quit altogether. But once you've seen the blood run dry from a hole you made in colder blood than you'd ever let on…

She looked him straight in the eye. "Don't give me reason to, then."

Piers returned to her car and drove off, ignoring the flicker in her headlights of Ack's silhouette against the rainfall. He hadn't moved an inch.

VII.

WHEN ACK ARRIVED at the door to Captain Liz Luciano's office, he could see that they were not alone. He paused on the other side of the frosted door, his hand on the handle, squinting at the second shadowy mass on the other side. He cursed to himself. There was no need to go in.

The door had barely clicked open when he started speaking, one finger raised in defiance. "Don't you dare try to tell me not to…"

"Shut up and sit down, Ack."

His finger curled into his fist, the door still held firmly in his other hand. He looked from Luciano, leaning against her desk, to Piers, sitting in a wooden chair, one hand rubbing her temple while the other held the chair's arm in a vise grip.

"I'll stand."

"Suit yourself."

Luciano paced before them, her hands clasped behind her back. She wore what looked like a pantsuit but what close observation would prove to be of a more elastic substance, designed for quick transition from business to a very different type of business, indeed. She made no attempt to conceal the weapon that hung from her hip, just as she applied her makeup carefully over everything but the jagged brown scar that cleaved the left half of her face in two.

When he'd first been called into Luciano's office as a young officer, Ack had faced her eye-to-eye, he in his painful wooden chair and she in her cushioned throne. She never sat anymore. Not since he'd started standing. He avoided eye contact, looking at a squirrel balancing on the dying branches of a pine tree. She stared at the side of his face until he could feel her dark brown eyes burrowing into his cheek.

"I don't like getting calls from the mayor, Ack."

He slammed the door shut. "I don't like being strongarmed out of investigating my case." He now turned to face her with a fire burning in his eyes.

She returned his look with fatigued impatience. "There's a right and a wrong way of doing things, and you know it. Or do we have to revisit the Giraud incident?"

"Giraud was guilty, *and you know it*."

"Beyond a reasonable doubt."

"Legal B.S. Reality is…"

"*Reality* is we need to follow that 'legal B.S.' even if we don't like it. And if we want to do anything about people like Giraud, we'd better make sure we don't do anything that'll let them walk."

"We were following a lead."

"Then, or yesterday?"

"Both."

Luciano scoffed and leaned back on her desk, looking to the sky in bemused wonderment. "You were investigating the shape of Giraud's imprint on your hood, I presume?"

Ack glowered.

"I'm not having a repeat."

"Fine. I'll let Piers drive."

"Leave me out of this." Piers raised her hands and pushed her chair closer to the window.

"Both of you are *very much* in this." Luciano turned from one to the other. Her tone softened. "You know there are things I would love to do—maybe things I even *did* back in the day—that you want to rush into right now. *But*—" she paused for effect "— actions have consequences."

"I think my third-grade teacher said that once."

"Fine. You know what, Ack, you want to go after a pair of upstanding citizens who've done more for this department—more for this *city*—than you could in ten lifetimes, you go right ahead and see what happens. But if you want to keep that desk—" Luciano jabbed a finger at the door "—and make any difference at all for the next twenty-five years, you'll learn when to cool off and shut your dumbass mouth."

It was Ack's turn to scoff. "Upstanding citizens?"

"What have they done, Ack? Name one *provable* thing they've done."

"I'm working on that. Or, at least, I *was* before you—"

"Finish that sentence."

"So, now you want me to open my—what was it, my 'dumbass mouth?'"

"I notice you didn't finish your sentence."

Ack said nothing.

121

"You know why that is? Because you actually *do* know what limits are, and we've just found one together. Now, I'm telling you another one. The mayor took a *very* unpleasant call from Hiram Hampburg last night while he was trying to have dinner with his family. I'll leave out the details about asses on pikes and defunded resources, but suffice it to say, the Hampburgs had better either be guilty as sin or never bothered again."

"They're guilty."

"On what evidence?"

"We'll find something," Piers said slowly, taking a deep breath more loudly than was necessary, like she was subconsciously trying to guide the rest of the room into a calm breathing pattern.

"When you do," Luciano began, pointing from one to the other. It was lost on none of them that she had said "when" and not "if." "When you do, I'll call the mayor, and we'll make things work from there. Until that time, I don't want to hear that either of you even *said* the name Hampburg outside this office. Am I clear?"

Ack looked to Piers. Piers shook her head.

"Fine." Ack opened the door.

"Yes, ma'am." Piers rose with a curt nod.

Luciano considered saying something more as they left the room but thought better of it. All in all, that had gone better than she'd expected. She crossed her arms and sat back on her desk, trying to will her heartbeat to calm. All the while, however, she couldn't help but draw her hand down the scar on her face, picturing that night, fifteen years earlier, when she and Hiram Hampburg had struck their unspoken deal that he would say nothing of her break and enter if she said nothing about the masks she'd seen in his basement.

"Hampburg!" Ack screamed through the shut door.

Luciano grimaced. She'd said that she hadn't wanted to hear that name spoken outside her office, but really, she'd hoped she would never hear it again.

VIII.

THE FENCE WAS marked with a series of rusty eight-by-twelve-inch signs reading "CAUTION: ELECTRICITY," but the Hunter knew better. They wouldn't risk it, not with the damage it could do if the crow flew carelessly in the night or dropped low in a gust. The crow was not impervious to pain. The Hunter had learned that the one time he'd come close, the day he'd acquired the scar that ate away a chunk of his left forearm. But he'd made the bird scream— that was the most important part of that failure.

The bird also became lethargic after a meal. He had seen it run on adrenaline and fight as though it was all-powerful, but just moments later it would dip in the sky, lose a few miles-per-hour off its speed. The bird was a beast, but at least in the earthly plane, it was fallible.

The Hunter had tested his theory with a squirrel. The creature hadn't heard him creeping through the trees. Silence was the Hunter's greatest skill. He'd taken the animal by the tail and flung it at the fence. The squirrel's limbs had spread widely and it had bounced once off the chains before grabbing on and slowing its fall. Most importantly, it had survived, unscathed. The Hunter had then retreated for five hours, unseen and unheard.

It was just after noon when he returned. He stationed himself behind a wide tree, dressed in brown to blend in with the trunks and dirt. What snow had made its way beneath the trees had largely been consumed by the rain of the previous night's storm. The ground was still damp; the trees dripped. There was no escaping the cold, but the Hunter didn't mind. He could sense the temperature. He had no fear of feeling it.

When he had found himself a covert spot, shielded by shadow from the view of the house, he finally felt comfortable facing the Hampburg manor. From the back, it was much plainer than it was from the front. One window. One door. All brick. It looked more like an unspectacular cottage than a mansion—or, it would have, if not for how high and wide it towered next to its neighbours.

The window was all the Hunter needed.

Straight ahead, he could see the cage. It was covered, but he could feel it moving. The beast never slept. Sometimes, it rested. But it never slept. The cover was thick and opaque, but the Hunter could see the shadow. He'd been trained to see even where light didn't penetrate. He'd once believed that to be impossible. They had taught him that "impossible" is a word designed by the strong to convince the weak that they've reached their peak.

The Hunter watched for over an hour, paying attention to patterns, assessing the creature's movements. He didn't want to imagine being trapped in a cage, alive but effectively nonexistent, for entire days.

What was the point in living if there was no control over life, movement, spirit? The Hunter smiled wanly to himself. He couldn't remember the last time he'd had full control. Still, the covered cage was something he wouldn't wish on his second-worst enemy. He couldn't say he wouldn't wish it on his first. He wished much, much worse on that crow.

The sun had crested the top of the sky and was beginning its descent straight through the window. This was the time he had been waiting for, when the crow would be blinded by the glare but his own sight would be perfect. The Hunter opened the thin, black pack on his back and assembled the shotgun. Poured his powder into the bullet. The Hunter lay with his stomach pressed against the damp dirt. Before he'd picked this spot, he'd spotted a groove in the ground, just below a tree root. He now rested the muzzle of the gun in that slot and adjusted his line until it was perfectly centred on the cage. The crow would be in his line in three…

Two…

One…

A crack from behind the Hunter made him jump. The gun lurched. His finger brushed across the trigger and it took all his force to keep from clenching on impact.

The Hunter rolled onto his back to face the intrusion, whipping the gun upward. Before he could aim it, a casual hand pressed it aside and held it firmly, leaving it pointed at nothing but the crown of a naked oak.

For a moment, the Hunter stared into Hiram Hampburg's eyes, each daring the other to make the

125

first move. It was the Hunter who struck first. He looked at the gun in hopes of distracting the old man, then kicked his leg into the back of Hiram's kneecap. He hadn't been quite as clever as he'd hoped. At the same moment, Hiram straightened his leg, pressing his knee back against the kick. It was a blow that still should have incapacitated even a strong, young man, but Hiram Hampburg knocked the kick away with ease. His facial expression never changed.

"Are you sure you want to do that?" Hiram's grip tightened on the gun and the Hunter felt certain he saw a dent in the metal.

"You don't understand what you've done," the Hunter said through gritted teeth. He fought off the pain spreading through his foot and spidering up his shin. It felt as though he'd kicked a slab of titanium, and the Hunter felt certain that the blow would have broken his foot. If his foot could have broken.

"It's a critical error to underestimate your opponent."

"You're not my opponent."

"You appear to be mistaken."

"Kill me then." The Hunter paused, a hard smile growing on his face. Even through the shadow that Hiram Hampburg cast across him, the Hunter knew the old man could see his expression. Hampburg swallowed. He hadn't meant for it to be seen, but the Hunter always saw. "You know you can't."

After a long pause, Hiram said, "You haven't heard the last from me."

He squeezed. The barrel of the gun crumpled in on itself, closing the chamber and leaving the tip pointed uselessly back at the Hunter.

The Hunter released.

Hiram dropped the weapon by his side. He turned without another look and started away, being sure to drive a heavy stomp into the Hunter's shin before he disappeared amongst the trees.

The Hunter lay still for a while, ignoring the pain that spread its tentacles across his entire lower half. He listened to the breeze whistle through bare branches and get caught in rustling pine needles. There were no footsteps. Just the sounds of nature going on in its endless cycle.

The Hunter stood and looked back at the house. He would be back. He would find a way. Undetected. Somehow. Though Hiram was always watching.

He turned to leave.

In the distance, the crow cawed.

IX.

THE PICTURES OF the crime scenes were eerily similar. Ack didn't know what he expected to find by pulling them up side-by-side, but he didn't have much else to go on. Not until the lab had finished with the rudimentary mould of the macaw's beak—which they'd assured him would be "useless" and "a waste of time."

"Jeez, Ack—you know we can't make anything remotely realistic from a blurry photo, right."

"Just do it."

"There's no point…"

"I don't care if it's a waste of time. Sitting here doing nothing is just as much of a waste."

"We have other cases to…"

127

"As important as a bunch of children being torn to shreds every day?"

Silence.

"That's what I thought. Make the damn moulds."

Ack zoomed in on the gashes and studied the flaps of serrated flesh, pulled at random angles, overlapping each other like they were being weaved into a basket. An empty basket.

"Dude, what the hell?"

Ack ignored it. Another in a long line of officers who'd made the mistake of walking past his computer as he glowered at the photos. If they couldn't handle a little blood, they were in the wrong line.

"There's a hell of a difference between murder and white-collar crime," Piers had once reminded him.

"Yes," Ack had replied. "One actually matters."

There was no pattern to the madness, no posing of the bodies, no hidden message. Ack scanned Li's notes for the twentieth time that morning.

The chest was always the first point of impact. The organs were removed. Tissue and bone between organs were sometimes eviscerated and sometimes left in perfect shape. That had led them to the conclusion that the assailant had enough medical knowledge to know precisely where he was looking but without any particular care for being gentle. By the violence and the blood flow patterns, Li suspected that the attacks were carried out rapidly, possibly within less than a minute…except that that would be impossible. There was no way to do that much damage with so small a tool in such a short period of time.

How a crow could have medical knowledge, Ack remained unsure. That a crow had done it and that the crow had some connection with that macaw, Ack was oddly certain. It was the absurdity that made it all too real. But it was equally the defensiveness of the Hampburgs. He supposed it was possible that they had performed the murders themselves, that their protection of the bird might have been related to their having fed it the organs or something of the sort. But then, two octogenarians violently gutting a body in just seconds seemed almost as insane as the crow theory.

"We have a name." Piers appeared at the side of Ack's desk. He didn't look up. "The anonymous witness. We traced the number. We have a name."

Ack hummed, still enthralled by the photos.

Piers looked away. The photos themselves she was used to, prepared for. The sight of Ack examining them so closely, totally unaffected by their perversity, was what made her feel sick. "You're gonna love this," she said, eyes closed. "His name's John Smith."

"Sure, it is."

"That's what I said. But that's what it's registered under and that's what we've got to go on."

"Address?"

"Can you look at me when I'm talking, at least?"

"I have a job to do."

She stopped herself from saying what was on her mind. Technically, he was right. She didn't have to like it, though. "No home address, but he rents an office on Valk Street. Called the security desk. Apparently, he's out a lot, but comes and goes at odd hours."

"And what, pray tell, constitutes an 'odd' hour?"

"Fine. An inconsistent schedule, if you'd prefer. And a lot more movement between two and six a.m. than you'd expect in a professional office building."

"I'm in here at three in the morning half the time."

"He's not a cop."

"What is he?"

"We don't know."

Finally, Ack looked up from his screen, but he didn't look at Piers. He was distracted by the window, by the cars flashing by in the distance, with sunlight flickering stars off their windows. A thought had hit him, but he wasn't sure what it was. Just that there was something strange eating at his mind, a concept of something greater than himself. It was as though the feeling had been projected to him.

But to draw him into danger or to protect him?

He couldn't be sure.

"Then, let's go find out."

X.

THE HUNTER SLIPPED quietly through the back-door of the building when a man from the third floor left. The fewer people who knew he was here, the better. Hiram Hampburg hadn't spared him that afternoon—he'd merely been unprepared. Most likely, Hampburg had spotted the Hunter from behind, just in time to save his precious bird. He'd been unarmed and without a plan. That wouldn't last for long. Hiram Hampburg hadn't survived unharmed for eighty-seven years by making a habit of letting his enemies walk away.

The Hunter avoided the security desk and stuck to the staircase, where he knew the cameras had stopped working months ago. He'd had a hand in that, in fact. In the early days of his preparation, he'd needed to maintain as much secrecy as possible. His presence would have been discovered eventually, but the less record there was of his movements, the better. There had been a pang of guilt when that young girl had been attacked there, but that hadn't stopped him from wiping out the next round of cameras just a day after they'd been installed.

It wasn't easy to climb eight flights of stairs with a heavy pack on his back, but the Hunter took the steps two at a time the whole way. There was no time to spare if he was going to be able to build his tools by tonight. Tonight might already be too late. There would be a rush now. The crow was nearly satiated, and Hiram knew that the Hunter was too near for comfort.

He slipped down the long hall, tiptoeing across carpet so thin it felt harder than linoleum beneath his shoes. He was silent, but was he swift enough? A figure moved behind a window to a conference room. No. Just the blink of a computer monitor's screensaver. The Hunter had no time to feel relief.

He shut the door to his office and flicked on the low, yellow light that made the room feel dark and heavy. A musty smell pervaded the small space, rising from the clothes that he'd piled around the corners of the room. The smell didn't matter—no one was ever near enough to notice. There was no money in his line. Funding came from mysterious sources.

The t-shirts that lined the walls doubled as insulation. Not for heat, which he couldn't feel, but for sound.

The Hunter commenced immediately, sweeping sheets and maps off his desk. He wouldn't need them anymore. He removed a series of powders and tools from the desk drawers and deposited them onto the newly cleared space. He worked by memory. It had been a long time since he'd faced the crow, but he remembered his steps and he remembered where he'd gone wrong. The gingerroot had been a glaring omission once before. The anthrax had been overdone. There had been other casualties. Not this time.

He mixed glue carefully with his powder and spread it across his weapon.

Then, he welded without protection. The desk caught fire. He patted it away with his bare hand. His forehead began to sweat. He could numb his sensations but his body still reacted.

The gadget, he finished last. It was the simplest of his tools and one which he could have purchased, if he could have brought himself to trust any source but himself. He'd done that once. Never again.

The finishing touches were in place. All that was left was for the glue to dry. Waiting. There was a strange serenity in waiting when the outcome was certain. There was only anguish when it was not. But what was it, the Hunter considered, when the outcome was certain to cause anguish?

Then, the waiting was nothing more than a microcosm of existence.

Life, wherein the end was always, undeniably, death.

But no—that wasn't the end, was it? For the individual, yes. For the consciousness.

But if death were truly the end, then he was a man without a motive or purpose. There was no good in saving a life only to have it die later on. His entire existence circulated around permanence—the piece of every life that could never disappear, but that could face the most excruciating of eternities.

No more, he promised himself.

No one else would suffer that fate under his watch.

Just a few more minutes and he would avenge the slain, disfigured bodies he'd mourned for decades. They would never know what he'd done. They would never thank him—no, he was too late for the ones who were already gone.

But for the ones who would never know what true suffering was—for them, he would act without any need for thanks. For them, he would assume every suffering the crow could bring.

There was a rustling in the hall.

The Hunter glanced at the final wet patch of glue, willing it to seal. A drill would have saved him—a drill would have been too loud. Another shuffle. There was no night janitor on this floor, just the ragged old man who pushed a squeaky-wheeled bin down the hall during the day, emptying trashcans with three Kleenexes inside.

He thought of the police—he hadn't made it hard to find him; he hadn't wanted to. They needed to know. He'd just hoped he would have solved their problems by now.

A louder step.

Not the police. Not at this time. Not just for a conversation.

That step was meant to startle him, to let him know that there was no time to escape.

The Hunter glanced at the window behind him. Eight storeys up and ten feet away from the fire escape. Could he make the jump?

When he turned back around, he found himself face-to-face with the barrel of a flamethrower.

His eyes flitted up to his assailant. Hiram Hampburg wore a blank expression, as though he was bored. Just another obstacle to be summarily disposed of. An inconvenience, rather than a life.

"It won't be enough." The Hunter swallowed.

"You're not the first. You won't be the last. I have means."

"We've gotten stronger."

"And so have I."

The Hunter took a slow breath. He'd been trained for moments like this. He could shut out the present and…yes…yes, he was okay. He was going to be okay, as he always was. He had the advantage in this tiny office. He knew precisely where the paint was peeling on the walls, which shirts sat in which corners, where the window latch was.

Hiram knew that, too, which was why he stood back, giving himself an additional split second to react. He wasn't far enough back, though.

Hiram's finger tightened on the trigger.

The Hunter's leg swept beneath the desk and connected with ankle.

It wasn't enough to do damage, but the unexpected bang vibrated the flamethrower an inch to the left.

A jet of flame singed the Hunter's ear. He didn't have time to see if he felt pain. He was already half-way to the window, tools in hand.

He anticipated the next jet, straight for his back, and snaked to the right. He could feel the glue coming unstuck between his fingers and he pinched tighter.

His arms full, the Hunter used his back to knock the window latch, to press the window halfway up. Then, he dropped quickly down to avoid another spray of flame. He didn't have time to open the window any further. His flesh be damned; he would slice it all off if it got him out of this room.

He only had one chance.

The Hunter sprang backward through the window and plummeted head-first toward the ground. He felt the tools fly above him. He could only pray they would fall on the grass. His hands gripped for a window ledge.

A jet of fire screeched past his left leg.

If he could just…latch…

A finger caught and scraped. Another.

The next ledge.

Another stream of flame.

His thumb clamped down. He was on.

The Hunter's fingers gripped the sill of a third storey window. His body flipped. His knee collided with the cement wall. He could deal with pain. He couldn't deal with the most recent shot from the window above.

The flamethrower had been enhanced for power and distance, but there was something else unusual about it. The smell of gingerroot.

Hiram knew.

135

The Hunter let go and braced for impact. The flame caught his shoulder.

He screamed out.

For the first time in decades, he felt heat.

The pain was excruciating. But he needed to remind himself that now wasn't the time for it. It was easier to ignore his knee, a simple bang. This cut deeper, into the root of his existence.

The Hunter hit the ground and raced for his tools, finding them miraculously unscathed. He scooped them up and didn't look back. He didn't need to. He could feel Hiram's presence growing nearer. He'd climbed down the wall. He approached.

A bolt of orange crossed the Hunter's periphery. He grunted at the burn against his shoulder. He hadn't remembered the pain of burning being so acute when he'd been nothing more than a man.

He still had the advantage of familiarity. He'd snuck through the backwoods to his office enough times. He knew the markings of the trees, the distance between fallen branches.

A left at the bird's nest, a right behind the knotted tree.

He was nearly at the stream that trickled a zigzag away from Lake Reamish when he first smelled the smoke.

For the first time since his escape, the Hunter turned to look upon the mess he'd left in his wake.

The forest had gone up in bitter flashes of orange and yellow, illuminating the void of the night sky. The birds screamed out. A squirrel raced past his feet, the fire on its tail quickly spreading to the rest of its fur.

The Hunter had no time to feel remorse for the desecrated nature. This was the doing of Hiram Hampburg. This was the fault of the crow.

The Hunter ducked into a cave, ignoring the bones beneath his soles, where a woman had once slept her final sleep.

He looked to his gadget, his capsules, his blade tipped with gingerroot and anthrax spores. He would wait here for the moment to pass.

He would not wait for long.

XI.

"I SAID WE should have come yesterday." Ack let a long, harsh flow of air escape his nose. He didn't look at Piers.

Piers closed her eyes. The moment she'd given Ack the information on "John Smith," she'd known it had been a mistake. He'd insisted on racing in, guns blazing, and shoving the anonymous man up against a wall until he'd squeezed the case out of him. It had taken stealing Ack's keys to keep him from violating protocol. Again. They'd only just touched the tip of the information trail.

"Would you rather have gone in blind?"

"As opposed to what? The treasure trove of information we know now?" A vein popped in his forehead.

"All I mean is, we *could* have found something useful. That was reason enough…"

"…to let everything go to Hell."

"Shut up, Ack."

He grunted.

Piers rolled her eyes. She knew that grunt too well. He'd get over it. He was going to be a petty bitch for a while first, though.

"Place looks like it's been ransacked," Piers said, looking around the small office.

When they'd arrived, the door had been ajar and creaking back and forth with every footstep down the hall. There was no point in knocking when they could see no one was home, but Piers had held Ack back and rapped twice, just to be sure.

There was barely room for the two of them in this small space. The rest of their crew were assigned to stand back and wait for a signal that would never come.

The word that came to Piers' mind, as she looked around the room, was "dying." It was messy but not dirty. It was cracking but not broken—yet. The walls were painted a sickly yellow that couldn't have ever been vibrant. They were now half-brown where the paint had peeled away, with a few stains and bubbles from years of condensation that had gone unwiped. The floors weren't in much better shape. Any lacquer that had once kept the hardwood looking clean and fresh had been scraped away, with some white lines left behind in its memory. There were a few scuff marks, but most of the damage was from scarring. Table legs that had been pulled a bit too hard, the wheels of a swivel chair. There was a desk in the centre of the room and a dusty desktop computer atop a cupboard that dug into the already limited space.

"Hasn't been ransacked," Ack grumbled, looking down at one of the many shirts that lined the edges of the room.

138

"How can you tell? There's crap all over the place."

"Not all over the place. Placed." He pointed at a few of the shirts. "Equal distance, pushed into the cracks, all touching the walls, nothing in the centre of the room. They were put here deliberately. Probably because this room is colder than a hobo on Christmas."

"You know—" Piers glared at him, knowing fully well that he knew "—my great-grandfather was homeless for two years after he got back from the war…"

"Was he cold on Christmas?"

Silence.

"Rest my case."

Piers refocussed her energy on something more winnable. "Fit these papers into your theory, then." She indicated the pile of loose-leaf sheets strewn around the desk."

Ack lowered himself slowly without bending his knees. After a moment, he said, "They were thrown there. Or pushed. But they weren't thrown at random. Might've blown in the wind a bit—" he gestured to the half-open window. "—but they're still all in the same place. Desk's empty. Looks to me like they were moved in a rush to clear a spot for something."

Piers did bend her knees as she lowered to get a better look at the table. "I'll get forensics to take a look into whatever this is." She pointed to a damp yellow patch. "Smells like…"

Ack grabbed her shoulder and yanked her back, catching a clump of her hair in the process. "Ow, what the hell?"

139

"Don't stick your nose into something when you don't know what it is."

"I'm not that much of an idiot," she said, rubbing her head gingerly. "I could smell it from where I was. And it smelled like ginger."

Ack didn't meet her gaze. "Next time, put a mask on and think before doing something stupid."

She scoffed. "You remember that next time you run into Sam Giraud."

He didn't respond.

Piers turned to the papers on the ground. "Raven rachis, toadstools, salamander tongue, root of lace-flower in brine…these papers read like a witch's brew."

"Check the computer."

"Without a warrant?"

"Didn't you hear a scream?"

"From the computer?"

Their eyes finally met in a harsh standoff.

Piers gave in first. "I'll walk by it and if my hand happens to brush the mouse, and the screen happens to come alive, then that really wasn't in our control, was it?"

The moment she stood up, she had regrets. The monitor was yellow but had once been white. Piers felt certain that it would be sticky to the touch. She didn't even want to brush the mouse with her elbow, let alone her fingertip. She pulled on a latex glove and squeezed her way around Ack.

The screen sprang to life. Or sputtered, hazing in and out, its twenty-years-out-of-date operating system clinging to the dying life of 1999. She didn't protest when Ack pushed her out of the way in his eagerness.

140

"Don't touch anything."

"Unlike you, I don't stick my nose quite literally where it doesn't belong."

He scanned the screen. It had opened to a document that displayed a series of numbers and letters that meant nothing to Ack. Piers glanced over his shoulder but quickly shook her head.

"What's that?" She pointed to a design in the top right corner of the document.

"Looks like fire." Ack pointed to the top left corner. "And that's water."

"Can we guess the bottom of the page is going to be air and earth?"

"The only thing we can guess is this guy's either a genius or a psycho."

"Says the guy who's blaming a series of violent murders on a bird?"

Ack hummed. "That might be the bit that makes the most sense."

Piers called for one of the other officers. Pitts had a penchant for codes and a nose for science. Piers suspected this might be his greatest challenge yet. With Ack showing no interest in leaving the room, Piers stepped aside to allow Pitts to enter. As he worked his brain in an exercise in futility, Piers began a rudimentary search of the "ingredients" she'd found on the office papers. She was on the phone with Bircham when Ack grumbled his way out of the office.

"We need a new analyst…"

Piers held up a finger to silence him. He stopped in the doorframe, leaving Pitts blocked in the room.

"Okay. Okay. Thanks." She hung up. "Got a lead."

Ack jerked a thumb over his shoulder. "Better than anything he's got."

"I need more time…" Pitts protested, but the others talked over him as though he wasn't there.

"Bircham's been looking into phone records. Looks like our friend 'John Smith' made a call to a novelty shop outside of town a few days ago, and credit card records have him making a purchase three days ago."

Ack's expression didn't change. "There's bad news."

Piers grimaced. For a man whose face never seemed to move, he had an annoying ability to pick up every small change in hers. "Whatever he bought—it was around the same time as one of the murders. Too far away for him to get back. Looks like he's not our guy."

Ack brushed past her. "He's something, all right. He might not be *the* guy. But he's something. And we're going to find out what. Now!"

Ack pushed past. Piers paused for a quick word with Pitts and another officer. Then, she followed down the hall. Ack didn't bother holding the elevator.

*

THE OUTSIDE OF Merlescu's fit perfectly with the rest of the street. The wooden sign was chipped and the red paint had faded with age and air. One of the windows was boarded up with a sign on it reading "Under Renovation." That sign, itself, needed renovations, with a scar across its face and one of its nails missing, leaving it hanging half off the wood. It wasn't a large façade, but the depth of darkness that spread behind the other window suggested that the place was deep. There were a few decorations in the window, all faded with age. A blackish cat figurine on the ground, a flying snake in the upper corner. A splash of graffiti had been painted over on the base of the building, but the edges of the green spray paint design still remained.

When Ack opened the door, a bell rattled but didn't ring. The clapper rolled away across the sticky hardwood floor when Ack's shoe caught it. It rolled under a glass display case that featured a gator's head and a range of grey teeth.

"Odds some of those are human?" Piers whispered.

Ack strode into the centre of the shop. The middle of the floor was poorly used, with nothing there but an empty table labelled "Display: Do Not Touch." The walls, however, were lined with glass cases, filled with a variety of objects. Behind the cases were shelves upon shelves of books and jars. Piers counted six organs in three seconds.

"Hello?" Ack called, not bothering to walk all the way to the back of the deep shop. Or maybe he just didn't want to walk into the darkness. The end of the store was shrouded in black.

"Come in; come forth," a low, hoarse voice replied.

An uncovered lightbulb flickered on in the distance, spraying a forty-watt halo over the head of the shopkeeper at the far end of the room.

"Does he stand there like that, waiting in the dark all day?" Piers murmured.

"Have you looked at him?"

143

"I'll take that as a 'yes.'"

As they neared, they realized just how small the man was. The glass case in front of him was lower than the others to make him appear taller, but he couldn't have been more than four-foot-nine. His skin was tight but white and pasty, as though he'd heard of the sun once but had no interest in learning more. His eyelids were thick and droopy, making him look like a horse wearing blinders. This image was only increased by his long chin and mane of white hair that stretched down the middle of his head but left the sides of it completely bald. His back arched in the middle. His knees bowed to the sides. He could have been anywhere from forty to two-hundred years old.

The detectives introduced themselves. The little man smiled as he shook their hands with a surprisingly tight grip for someone whose fingers resembled bones. "Roy Straddler."

Ack shook his head. The name was too normal for a man who was so…not. "Who's Merlescu?" he asked.

Straddler grinned. "How can I help you, detectives?"

"Who's…" Ack started, but Piers cut him off.

"We're looking for information about a man who we believe came into your shop on Monday around three in the afternoon. Were you here that day?"

"Naturally. I never leave."

"*That*, I believe," Ack muttered. Piers elbowed him in the ribs.

She continued, "Do you remember the customers you had that day?"

"Naturally," he said again. "There was only one. Only one for quite some time."

"How the hell's a place like this stay open, anyhow?" Ack gazed around at the phials and jars, his eyes fixating on what he felt almost certain to be a human heart.

"It's a pig's heart, detective," Straddler said, reading his mind. "And let's just say that, when you're needed, the world finds a way."

"Let's just say some real answers."

"Ideally—" Piers edged her shoulder in front of Ack, getting the overwhelming sense that he wanted to lunge at the little man, if just for something to do "—related to the customer you had a few days ago. Do you remember anything about him? What he looked like; what he bought?"

Straddler raised a finger with a small smile and turned to the cabinet behind him. He rifled around until he found a large, dusty binder. He didn't bother to wipe it off. He plunked it on the table in front of him with a loud crack and plied the pages apart one by one, murmuring to himself the whole time. Piers could sense Ack's jaw tightening, his shoulders driving forward. She held up a hand to silence him.

"Ah yes, here it is. Mr. Smith purchased gingerroot, rachis of raven, twelve toadstools, tongue of salamander, root of laceflower in brine, spores, gel capsules, and a pinch of mammoth dust, but I suspect that's for himself."

"Smith's his real name, do you know?"

Straddler smiled again. "What is a name, really?"

"So, no."

"I couldn't tell you if I wanted to. But, by the grace of the Lord, I have nothing to tell."

"What's that supposed to mean?" said Ack.

"There are things better left unsaid."

"Not right now, there aren't."

"Testy, testy."

"Let's…just stick to the facts," Piers said, trying not to make her sharp glance at Ack too obvious to the other man. "What does this Smith look like?"

"Like you and me."

"We don't look alike, buddy." Ack pressed in front of Piers' shoulder. "Hell, no one looks like you."

Straddler seemed to feed off the energy, his smile only growing. "What I mean to say is, he looks like anybody. You wouldn't know him on the street, even if you knew him."

"This is a waste of our time." Ack turned back to the heart of the room, waiting for Piers to follow.

"Just one more question, before we go, Mr. Straddler."

"Anything for a lovely lady."

Piers grimaced. Straddler appeared to enjoy it.

"What would Mr. Smith be doing with that list of…are they ingredients?"

"Oh, yes. Most definitely."

"For a…potion of some kind?"

"No," Straddler laughed. It was a sharp, ringing laugh that felt like daggers thrown at the walls. "A powder, a rub, perhaps a cream, but not a potion."

"And what might he intend on doing with something like that?"

Straddler's brow furrowed. He turned from Piers to the back of Ack's head, a glimmer of knowing in his eye mixed with genuine confusion. "You don't know? Detectives," his voice turned stern, "if you don't know…there are things you oughtn't face blind. We're speaking of genuine evil here. A possession most…fowl. Stay away, while you still have the chance."

Ack wheeled about, his voice booming around the cavernous shop. "Don't hide anything from us, or I'll have your shop shut down for the foreseeable future. Don't think I won't."

"That would be in nobody's best interest, Detective."

"In that case, answer the damn question. What the hell's this guy going to do with those ingredients?"

Straddler paused for a moment, took a breath. "Naturally," he said, "he's going to murder the crow."

XII.

"NO. A MILLION times and a million times again: no!"

Luciano slammed the receiver down on her home phone and pinched the bridge of her nose. It was one thing for Ack to call her on her day off. Another to call after nine p.m. And another altogether to call about the very thing she'd warned him to stay away from. She eased herself into a blue armchair next to the phone and shook her head slowly. The migraine would pass—they always did. If she could just keep a little peace and quiet for a few moments…

"Mommy! Play baseball!"

"Not now, Jackson," she said, glancing up quickly and immediately regretting it. The low, yellow light in the dining room felt like the sun hanging over the little boy's head.

Jackson's long, curly hair bobbed up and down as he threw a baseball in the air and tried to catch it. He missed—he always missed—and it thudded hard against the ground. Luciano winced.

She'd never gotten even minor headaches before the Hampburgs had messed up her head, and something had always told her that Lo had had something to do with that, the powders she mixed in the corner as Hiram held Luciano around the neck. She'd done something to her.

"Baseball, Mommy!"

"I said, 'Not now!'" she snapped.

His face went slack.

Luciano forced her eyes open to look at the hurt, open-mouthed expression of her son. The boy was barely four and she felt like she hardly knew him, what with long working hours and early-morning paperwork. The nanny was more the boy's mother. At least Liz was still better than his father, who wanted nothing to do with his son. "I have work," had been Morris' excuse. Sometimes, though she refused to admit it aloud, in the middle of the night, she felt the same.

"I'm sorry, baby," she said, the word 'baby' sounding cold and forced in her mouth. "Mommy has a headache. We can play on the weekend. Okay?"

"So far away!" The boy's back arched and his head turned to the sky. He started to cry, his wails only making Luciano's head pound more. She forced herself up to give the boy a gentle pat on the back.

"It's okay, honey…" No, 'honey' didn't sound any better. "It'll be here before you know it. Just go play on your own. Maybe play on the computer or in the basement, okay?" She hesitated, not wanting to make a promise she couldn't keep. But one look at his red, scrunched up face had her prioritizing quiet peace over truth. "If I feel better, I'll come play with you later."

Jackson sniffled. He rubbed his hand against his nose and looked at the snot. He wiped it on Luciano's trackpants. "O-okay," he said. He waited for a minute, probably hoping for a hug or a kiss or maybe even a scolding. Anything to buy him a few more minutes in the room. But Luciano had no clue what kids wanted. Jackson had been an accident—a 'happy accident,' she'd said so many times she'd started to believe it. She patted him on top of his brown curls and turned his shoulders around. With a pat on the bum, he was on his way.

A few thuds on the stairs past the back door. And then there was silence.

She collapsed back in the chair, trying not to think.

But all her head would do was replay her conversation with Ack.

"He's going to kill the crow. The guy said he's going to kill the crow."

"There's no crow."

"I'll be damned if that's a real macaw."

"Are you even hearing yourself, Ack? You sound like a madman. Now, shut up and stay away from the Hampburgs."

"It's going to be on you when another kid gets tartared."

149

"Then find me some real evidence, why don't you?"

"What more do you need?"

"Something more interesting than an old wives' tale."

"Could be your kid next, Liz. Ever think about that?"

"Never say that again! Don't be looking forward to tomorrow, Ack. I swear to God, you don't *want tomorrow morning to come, right now."*

"He called it a possession, Liz. I've heard about these things before."

"In a horror movie?"

"No. A kid in Caprice. Look—I don't know all the details. Not my job."

"By which you mean, you don't like not knowing, so you'll pretend you just don't care, instead?"

Silence. "It ended badly, Liz. For everyone."

"Fairy stories."

"If these are the fairies, we don't want to know the demons."

A pause. A grunt. "Just leave the Hampburgs alone. And leave me the hell alone, too, while you're at it."

He'd kept protesting.

That was when she'd slammed the receiver down. She wanted to put it out of her head. It was ridiculous. It was pseudoscientific, supernatural B.S.

Which was also precisely what she'd called the crow all those years ago…

Luciano closed her eyes and tried to sleep, pulling a hand over her eyes so she wouldn't have to get up and walk all the way to the light switch. It was no good. The crow flew out of the blackness on the inside of her eyelids, its beak a flicker of grey snapping at her face.

The kid in Caprice. She'd heard about that. At the time, she'd wondered. Poked into some disreputable journals to find out more. Articles by no-name fantasists like "Daniel Reese" and "Ogilvie Thorpe." It was all cant and bull.

Still, the thought stuck with her.

A gust of cold air finally distracted her from her condition. She breathed it in slowly. There was nothing better than winter air for making her feel at peace. Her body felt refreshed, clean, new. She felt like a young woman again, just waking up to the world she wanted to live in instead of the one she'd found.

She took another deep breath. Her migraine was nearly gone. Or maybe she just couldn't feel it anymore now that her body had been renewed.

Despite the peace, though, there was still something roiling in her gut. Something was wrong. The house was well-sealed. She'd just had the walls patched and insulated a few months earlier. The windows were closed to keep the draughts out, to keep them from getting sick, to keep them from wasting money on an electricity bill that had only gotten higher every year since Jackson had entered her life.

All the refreshing life that had just seeped into her body evacuated like a trapdoor had been pulled open from her back. For a moment, she was sucked back into the chair. Then, she was empty to the point of feeling hollow, shaking as she stood.

The back door was open. She could hear it banging.

151

Jackson.

The murderer.

If Luciano's stomach hadn't already left her, it would've dragged her to her knees in that moment.

She vaulted for the door, her socks sliding across the hardwood floor, pulling her further from her destination. She didn't have time for shoes or a jacket. She raced through the open door and into the backyard.

There was Jackson, standing in the heart of the yard in nothing but his pyjamas, looking up at the sky, mesmerized. But alive. He was alive. She could see his chest rising and falling.

"Jackson!" She ran for him, reaching out to grab him. The snow was still deep in her yard. No trees around. Fully exposed to the elements. It was impossible to believe that Jackson had made his way so far into the yard already. Being as light as he was, he'd barely made a dent in the hard, icy snow.

Luciano sank with every step.

"Jackson!"

"What's colour?" he said, pointing up.

"I don't know, honey," she choked out that unusual word. "Just come back inside, please." She took another step. The cold was already seeping into her flesh. Why wouldn't he just turn around and make this easier on her?

"Mommy, what's colour?"

Luciano's fist clenched. Now that she knew he was safe, her number one priority was getting out of this cold and into the warm embrace of the house. She realized the door was open behind her, wasting even more heat.

"Jackson…!"

"What's colour?"

Her shoulders tensed, her eyes ready to pop out of her skull. Luciano growled as she looked up at the sky and followed Jackson's finger.

Her body slackened. There was a streak of colour up there, circling. She frowned. What *was*…?

There was no time to complete the thought. The rainbow figure plummeted so quickly that it looked like barely more than a line cleaving the sky in half. Luciano just registered the macaw before it turned jet black, and the crow plunged straight into Jackson's heart.

"No!" she cried out, trying to race forward. But there was no way to get there in time. In seconds, the bird had torn the boy's chest to shreds, painting blood and flesh and flecks of bone across the glimmering white of the snow.

Jackson fell back, completely still, a chasm in his chest. His face was frozen as though he'd lain there the whole night. Luciano stared down at the hole of his empty chest, blacker than the night sky.

The crow hung in the air, watching. "I'll kill you!" she screamed, lunging for the bird.

Her foot caught on the lip of the ice. Luciano sailed face-first into the snow, just inches from where her dead son lay.

"I'll kill y…"

The moment her face rose, the crow was there. Its talon pierced through her tongue and tore it from her head. Blood began to fill her throat. She couldn't breathe.

The bird attacked again, its beak pecking at her eyes, plunging toward her brain.

"Stop!"

She heard the cry coming from the distance.

She knew it was too late.

The last thing she heard was a deep, booming battle cry.

The Hunter slid across the ice, focussing his weight into his upper body in a way that only he could. He, too, knew that he would be too late to save the woman or the child. The boy had already been gutted. The woman's face had been shredded. The crow turned to face him, a glob of gooey brain matter dripping from its beak.

The Hunter swung his blade for the bird. It flapped its wings.

It dipped.

The blade just missed, but the Hunter had learned what he needed to know. The crow was fatigued. It had consumed its lifeblood and now it needed time to rest.

He swung the blade again and the crow barely dodged, trying to find its strength. It headed for the Hunter's side. It wanted to fly circles around him, to keep him guessing.

It wouldn't have to.

"No!" the Hunter cried, yanking at his blade. It was lodged in the thick snow. It wouldn't come out.

The bird flew for his face.

The Hunter dove back in time to avoid the worst of the damage, but he felt the flesh tear on his cheek.

He scrambled to his feet above the ice and looked from the bird, flying a few feet to his left, to the blade, lodged in the ground to his right. There was no time. The crow flew for him. The Hunter reached forward.

At the last moment, the crow saw the gadget in the Hunter's hand. Too small to be seen by the Hampburgs in the morning. Impossible for the bird to remove by itself.

At the last moment, it veered, trying to avoid the Hunter and pursue the safety of home.

The Hunter didn't know if the bird felt him. It must not have, because it kept going, rising into the blackness of the night until it was invisible in the sky.

But he'd succeeded in part. The gadget was attached. It was only a matter of time.

The Hunter wiped a drop of blood from his cheek as he stepped toward the fallen mother and son. As he'd feared, both were well beyond saving.

She kept herself, though, he thought. *At least, she kept her eternity.*

The same couldn't be said for the boy. He was one with the crow now.

Was it a greater tragedy to be the victim of an evil cause or to die for nothing?

It didn't matter, the Hunter supposed.

Both were gone.

He thanked them silently. They had given themselves for his benefit, and he would be forever grateful.

So long as the bird needed one more meal, the Hunter would accomplish his goal and destroy the beast.

He calculated slowly, going over the numbers—just the ones he knew about. If there had been any more…he couldn't think about that. He needed to hope the crow had one last feed in him. If not…

If not…it would be a long wait before he could continue the chase.

XIII.

"I'M DRIVING."

"Not a chance in hell."

Ack bodied Piers out of the way and had the key in the ignition before she had gotten to the car. Locking the driver's side door would have seemed almost childish if not for the murderous expression etched across his face.

Piers tried the door a few times, screamed something incoherent. She glowered at him as she dropped into the passenger's seat.

"Give me the keys. Now." She held out her hand but knew it was pointless. Ack started driving while her door was still half-open. "Come on, Ack. You didn't even like Luciano. What's with the sudden action-hero charade?"

Piers regretted speaking the moment Ack pulled his eyes from the road to glare at her. "Who says I didn't like her?"

Piers blinked. She'd expected yelling, cursing, even the silent treatment. Not this. Her outstretched hand involuntarily started to close on itself. "Every time you talked to her—every time you talked *about* her…Can you please look at the damn road?"

Ack turned just in time to swerve away from an oncoming green punch buggy. He ignored the extended horn behind him and turned back to Piers as

156

though he hadn't just been driving in the wrong lane. "You *do* understand the difference between arguing and hating."

"I wasn't sure you did."

"Yes-men don't get anywhere. There's a reason you fight for what you believe in. Sometimes, you're right. And sometimes, being wrong means you die. Case in point." He jabbed a thumb over his shoulder that Piers wished he would keep on the wheel, but at least he'd turned back to the road.

Piers sank down in her chair. "The mayor's not going to like this," she mumbled.

"He's also not going to like what just happened to his chief of police."

Piers checked her messages. "It was 'Smith' who called it in again. That's a more suspicious lead than a bird. Safer place to start, at least."

"Playing it safe is what got us to this point." He let that sit for a minute before continuing, "And you heard what the neighbour said."

There was nothing for Piers to say to that. "John Smith" had been the first to call in Luciano and Jackson's violent murders, but he hadn't been the only one. The next-door neighbour, a seventy-two-year-old woman named Shirly Macombe, had heard the yells "No!" and "Stop!" but had attributed them to the TV. Old Mr. Jon Macombe was always watching that old idiot box, never stopped watching even after...he'd died, she'd suddenly remembered. He'd died fifteen years earlier in a car crash while driving home drunk from his retirement party. And if those screams hadn't come from a TV that hadn't worked in eighteen months, when her son had steadfastly refused to

157

fix any more of her various technological foibles until she learned to help herself—if those screams hadn't come from the dead old idiot box, well then, they must have come from outside!

By the time she'd reached the back window and cautiously peeked out from beneath blinds that she always kept shut, it was too late to do anything to help. The boy had looked like a black hole that would suck you straight into the earth and the mother was lying face down, like she'd drowned in a swimming pool of her own blood. There had been a man with a blade, swinging wildly at what she'd first believed to be nothing, but soon realized was a bird that had blended with the night sky.

Piers had focussed on the man with a weapon.

Ack had focussed on the crow.

"I wish I could unsee all of that," Piers said, gazing out the window. There was no point in telling Ack, but she didn't care. In that moment, she needed to expel one of the harsh, sickening emotions from her system and he was just going to have to live with that.

"Then, you're in the wrong line."

"You're heartless."

"I'm realistic."

"There are good things in reality, too, Ack. Just because you've never seen any of them…"

"Don't tell me I've never seen a good thing. I've seen good things. Every one of them slips away or dies. So, like I said, I'm realistic."

"You sorry sonofabitch."

"You're half right. I'm a sonofabitch, but I'm sure as hell not sorry about it."

158

He pulled the car to an abrupt stop outside the Hampburg estate.

"They won't let us in," Piers said.

"They did last time."

"Then immediately called the mayor."

"Only reason they don't let us in is they're guilty."

"Try that one in a court of law, see how it pans out."

"Tried that." Images of Sam Giraud flickered across his mind in varying shades of red. "Won't make the same mistake twice."

Piers' eyes opened wide; her heartbeat increased until her body became numb. "Oh God, Ack. What're you going to do?"

Ack was already out of the car and halfway to the house.

Piers scrabbled at her seatbelt, realizing for the first time that Ack hadn't bothered with his. She didn't waste time with closing the car door behind her. She raced to cut Ack off.

But he'd already knocked.

"Don't do it."

"Don't do what?"

"Whatever you're thinking. It can only go badly."

"I'm *thinking* about getting answers."

"If you lay a hand on him…"

The heavy door creaked a fraction of an inch. A few more.

The shadowed face of Hiram Hampburg appeared. He didn't blink. His gaze was flat, but there was distaste in his eyes. His mouth was a cold, thin line. "Detectives."

"Where's the crow, Hiram?" Ack's hand hit the door, but it was too heavy to move more than an inch, even with a punishing blow.

"If you find a *crow* on our property, I assure you it's as much of an intruder as you are. And, if you please, I don't believe we're quite on a first-name basis, *Detective Ackersley*."

"I know what you've done."

For a moment, Hiram paused. His eyes traced up and down the detective's body, considering, as a smile crept onto the corners of his lips. "No. No, I don't believe you could possibly know anything at all."

"What's that supposed to mean?"

The smile had grown into a smirk. Hiram Hampburg stepped aside. "Come find your crow, detectives. Be as thorough as you'd like. I insist." He disappeared into the shadows.

"Don't go in there," Piers hissed.

"It's an invitation," Ack said, but still he didn't move. His fire had temporarily reduced. He didn't know what he was going to find inside, but he was certain that he wouldn't like it.

"Come, please. It's time."

Piers glanced to Ack. He hesitated, then looked back. She could see something waver in his eyes. He swallowed. As his Adam's apple bulged up, then down, it tightened his body, his shoulders, his chest. Ack closed his eyes and, when he opened them again, the fire had returned, although not with nearly as much heat as before.

He pressed open the door.

Piers sighed and followed, although she maintained a defensive posture with each passing step.

The hall felt brighter today, like life had been breathed back into this place. Even the dust had a glow around it, a yellow halo instead of a dead, grey disaster.

Lola Hampburg sat in her same position on the couch, facing the covered bell on the table at the far side of the room. She didn't look up at the detectives. On her lap were a pair of knitting needles and a spool of yarn, but no progress had begun on whatever she was making. She hummed quietly to herself, a tune Ack remembered from his childhood. A church hymn. Without the choir it sounded hollow and empty.

Ack made straight for the birdcage. Piers remained at the door, her hand inching closer to her weapon. She had no intention of using it. She just needed to know that it was there. A safety net.

If she needed to run, she would never be able to open that door in time to escape an attack. She tried not to think about that. Her eyes flitted from Ack to Hiram, standing beside the fireplace, to Lola, humming away. Ack's hand pinched around the cloth of the birdcage. A small cry escaped Piers' throat. Lola's humming got louder. Hiram grinned.

The sheet fell away and beneath, Ack found…

…nothing.

An empty cage.

No food.

No droppings.

No water.

No bird.

161

He stared for a moment, as though he could have missed a large animal at first glance. Ack slowly turned to face Hiram Hampburg, his neck and head bent low, a growing hatred in his eyes. Hiram merely smiled.

"Satisfied, detective?"

"Where's. The. Bird?"

"I fear that our poor macaw is away for...treatment."

"Not the damn macaw. The crow. Where's the damn crow?"

"As I told you at the door, detective: there's no crow here. There never was."

Ack seethed.

"If you'd like to search the rest of the house..."

Ack didn't say a word. He knocked into Piers as he made for the door. She took one last look from the old man to the old woman. Lola's humming dropped. Hiram's smile turned into a sneer.

"Th...thank you for your time," Piers said quietly. She rushed to follow.

"Not at all, detectives," Hiram called after them. "We appreciate your concern for our poor bird. But I assure you, he's quite well. And he *will* be back."

Ack didn't bother closing the door on his way out. He stormed across the lawn, straight for the car.

"Ack! Ack! What the hell was that?" Piers burst in front of him and used both hands to block him on the sidewalk. "The mayor's going to have your head, now."

"If the mayor wants it, he can have it. As long as theirs are rolling first."

"If they're guilty, we'll get them. But we have to do it the right way or they're just going to walk. And we *know* they'll walk with a vengeance."

"That was a threat and you know it—on the way out. 'He *will* be back.' That was a threat."

"No—" came a voice from behind "—it's a stark reality that we're all going to have to accept and that I will have to deal with. But it's nothing for you to worry about."

Piers jumped. Ack tensed but held his ground. They both turned to face the man approaching slowly from the end of the street. He wore a black overcoat and a grey fedora. His hands were in his pockets. It was his face that struck Piers the most. The man was almost entirely plain. If she'd had to describe him for a police sketch, she imagined she would come up with little more than a stick figure with a 1940s aesthetic.

"And who the hell are you?" Ack asked, but he knew. They all knew that he knew.

"Take your hands out of your pockets slowly." Piers' hand returned to the bulge at her side.

The man complied, raising two black-gloved hands halfway to the sky. He smiled a weak, little smile.

"I apologize for my cryptic messages. The less you knew, the safer you'd be."

Piers swallowed. "Then, why send them at all?"

"No good in being on the wrong track. At least you knew what you couldn't prove."

"You're Smith." It wasn't a question.

The Hunter smiled wanly. "What is a name, really?"

"We have some questions for you, Smith, and it would do you well to answer them," Ack snarled.

"In due course, you'll know all. For the time being, you'll know what you need to."

Ack opened his mouth to speak, but the Hunter raised his hand.

"This is what I know. You are safe. We're all safe. For now. The crow is finished feeding for this cycle and has returned to some other hellish plane. I counted the bodies—I must have missed one. Perhaps an animal, a dog or cat. Whatever the case, we were too late—*I* was too late. The bird will return, but not for some time yet. When its lifeblood wavers; when its keepers need strength to carry on. But you can rest assured that the children of Reamish are no longer in danger."

"And when will this so-called *cycle* start again?"

"You can trust me, detectives, that it will not. My chase continues. But I *will* destroy the bird before you ever need to fear it again. You can hold me to that, detectives. In thirty-two years when no children have died, you will know that I've ended the threat."

"Like you did this time," Ack spat, taking a step forward. "Just who and *what* are you?"

The Hunter smiled again. "I ask myself the same thing every morning when I wake up and every night before I go to bed. You know what my answer is? A failure. I've failed time and time again. But, equally, I'm persistent. And until the day that bird and its brethren have been slain, I will continue to fight."

"I—I don't understand," Piers said. "What is it? What is this 'bird' you're talking about? Because no bird did what happened to those kids. How do we know *you* aren't our killer."

The Hunter took a slow, deep breath. He didn't answer. He looked up at the Hampburg estate and instead said, "Look at what they've done for their youth and their strength. I wish I could say they were the only ones…

"…the race is done…

"…the night wind's committed its evils…

"…the bodies are buried in the snow…

"…and now the crow is gone." He turned to face the detectives. "The darkness will come to Reamish again. It cannot be stopped. But I will do my utmost to mute it. This, I promise you."

He turned and retreated down the street at a slow, laborious pace. The weight of a hundred-thousand deaths pressed on the Hunter's back, scalding the burn that would never leave his shoulder. But he didn't stop. He never would.

It took a stunned moment before Ack and Piers realized that their prime suspect was disappearing without really having told them anything at all.

Ack broke for the man first with Piers following closely behind. He rounded a corner behind a tall hedge. Ack skidded to a stop at the edge of the sidewalk and continued in pursuit.

He grabbed the shoulder of the black overcoat just as Piers arrived behind him.

When Ack spun the man around, he and Piers stared, open-mouthed. For a moment, Ack would not let go.

It was Piers who broke the stunned silence. "I'm sorry for my partner," she said. "We've made a mistake."

Ack released, but his hand remained frozen in place. The one-eyed man with a cleft lip and a series of moles down the side of his face nodded without a word and turned back on his way.

"Where…where the hell did he go?" Ack's voice became softer with each passing word.

The detectives turned about. There was nowhere to hide. Nowhere to disappear to. Not in such a short period of time. Yet, "John Smith" was gone.

The one-eyed man smiled gently to himself as he walked away. Within a moment, his face had morphed back to the unrecognizable blandness of the Hunter. The curse he shared with the crow. The thing that made him just as awful as the very things he sought to destroy.

The Hunter removed the tracker from his pocket and watched the radar map flicker. He'd failed to catch the crow, but it had been marked with his tracker. Indeed, it had been too small for the Hampburgs to notice.

For now, the bird was gone, beyond any realm that he could access. But it would be back. And the moment that it returned to Earth, he would be ready. He fingered the blade in his other pocket. He would be ready, and this time, he would kill before the beast could strike.

In the meantime, there were other birds.

How he wished there could be just one.

But there was nothing unique about the Hampburg crow.

About the Author

Scott R.S. Raphael

Scott R.S. Raphael is a Canadian author and poet based out of Toronto. He holds a B.A. in English and Cinema Studies from the University of Toronto. Raphael has been writing fiction and making art since he was seven years old. He entered the public eye in 2019 when he began posting selections of his poetry on Instagram. Principally an author of fiction, with particular focus on the horror and fantasy genres, Raphael has written a diverse collection of novels and short stories.

Connect with Scott at:
https://scottrsraphael.com/
Twitter/TikTok/X: @scottrsraphael
Instagram: @srsraphael

Other Works by Scott R.S. Raphael

SPRUCE ROAD

The Little Maple Cabin on Spruce Road is the perfect place for an escape from city life. Hidden away in the middle of nowhere, in a forest, along winding roads, it's beautiful, pristine, and quiet. Almost too quiet.

When a group of young friends decides to get away for a birthday celebration, they expect a weekend of drinking, partying, and relaxing by the fire. They don't even have to be careful with their volume, as their closest neighbour—the Cottage's mysterious owner—is two miles down the road. Their closest *living* neighbour, anyway.

When their host warns them of a ghostly presence in the home, most don't take him seriously but, when mysterious things start happening, the group is forced to search for answers...

...and pray that they live long enough to find them...

ASHER'S PALACE

A year has passed since the events of Spruce Road, and the mystery of the partygoers' deaths remains unsolved. Back at Asher's Palace, the upscale restaurant where most of the victims had once worked, life goes on as usual.

Nick Whitley, a congenial server who doesn't take his job as seriously as some of his managers would like, spends his days pleasing customers, chatting with co-workers, and flirting with Danielle, a charming but fiery cook with a criminal past. The pleasant monotony of his world is turned upside down when he's visited by the ghost of a friend who had met his end a year earlier. A friend who comes with a mysterious warning.

Meanwhile, Nick's co-workers discover that their grand, historic restaurant hides secrets within its high, impressive, but peeling walls. The ghosts of the people who had once called Asher's Palace home start appearing in the stairwells, the kitchen, the dining hall after dark. These horrors are only heightened by the appearance of a mysterious man who warns Nick that there is unfinished business at The Little Maple Cabin on Spruce Road.

With danger and death staring them down, a group of staff members at Asher's Palace are forced together to pursue answers about what really happened to their murdered friends. But at the same time, something sinister is pursuing them...

A LITTLE SLICE

Emily Dresden was a normal high schooler. Popular, fun, a good student, a kind-hearted person who was looking forward to the future. So, no one can quite figure out why she tried to kill herself last September. Including Emily.

Now back at school after a long recovery, she's cut herself off from her old friends, including her best friend, Daniel, who's determined to help Emily get back to normal. But Emily doesn't think that she can ever be normal again. Not because she doesn't want to be, but because she's convinced that there's something evil inside her, warping her mind and endangering those closest to her. And clawing to get out...

WARNING: A Little Slice contains themes of death, suicide, self-harm, and mental illness, and is recommended for adult readers.

TAKE YOUR LIFE

Michael has always prioritized the happiness of the people in his life. So, naturally, he's devastated when his close friend and colleague Hannah is passed up for promotion, despite his best efforts to sway the board of directors in her favour. Michael does his best to console his frustrated friend and to encourage her to keep up the hard work until her day finally comes.

Hannah seems to have other ideas.

When the members of the board of directors start to meet unfortunate fates, Michael doesn't want to believe that Hannah is involved, but the thought just won't leave his head.

Along with the fear that he could be next...

STREAKS OF DESCENT

Battle is first fought within.

Two painters, Tom Wainwright and Henry Tulack, have captured the adoration of the modern art world but have no respect for each other's work. In fact, they have no respect for each other, at all.

When they are retained as co-headliners for an up-coming charity gallery, their desire to outdo one an-other comes to a head, and the painters impulsively challenge each other to produce a new painting in the other's style in less than a month.

But before they can understand what makes their rival tick, they must first battle their own shortcomings.

THE FIFTH PASSENGER; AND OTHER PERVERSITIES

Nine tales of the strange and uncomfortable. Nine stories marked by the darkness of perversity. Unusual tasks and unusual people; decisions, divisions, and nightmarish landscapes. The Fifth Passenger and Other Perversities contains a selection of never-be-fore-published stories from the twisted depths of the mind of Scott R.S. Raphael.

CERTAINTY; AND OTHER MISTAKES

Broken people, vengeance, life, death, and that which comes thereafter define this collection of short stories from the twisted mind of Scott R.S. Raphael, author of *A Little Slice* and *Spruce Road*.

From horror to mystery to crime to...comedy?...*Certainty and Other Mistakes* includes eight strange and discomforting tales of darkness and distress.

Includes the novella "Cutaneous"!

THE HILL AT THE TOP OF THE MOUNTAIN

Harper Gale is a bestselling author, haunted by the ghost of her recently-deceased husband, and terrorized at work by her disrespectful superior.

Tristan Ames is a rock star, haunted by a dark secret from his past, and terrorized by his bandmates as he struggles to write music again.

Their connection is immediate, but will their personal demons, emotional instability, and fear of moving forward keep them apart?

BEING ON THE ISTHMUS OF RAGE AND DESPAIR

"...being on the isthmus of rage and despair/all I can do is stand, and sit, and stare."

In his debut poetry collection, Scott R.S. Raphael explores the depths of the human mind through a narrator battling the throes of unrequited love, fear, death,

172

fantasy, mental deterioration, and, of course, rage and despair.

An exploration of the human condition and the depths to which one can sink within the darkest corners of the mind, *Being on the Isthmus of Rage and Despair* reaches into what it means to live and seeks the answers sought by many but captured by few.

"*I miss you*/ And I reply,/*I do too*/But I'm not sure if I'm referring to her/or to myself,/for both are equally gone"

A GLASS FOR LOVE, HATE, AND THE PERPETUAL PARTY

You are born. The party is already raging.
You are aging. The party has taken over.
You are dying. The party makes one final push.
You are gone. The party toasts your exit.

A Glass for Love, Hate, and the Perpetual Party is a poetry collection for those in the heart of the celebration, whether they want to be or not.

Printed in Great Britain
by Amazon